Rowan has been alone since his family died, and he wants to keep things this way. He's not willing to care about someone else and have them ripped away from him. His heart wouldn't survive it.

Clay has been alone since his family died, but when he sees Rowan working at the bar where he's hunting a Kudlak, he can't stay away, doubly so after Rowan saves him from the Kudlak and tells him they're mates.

Hunting Kudlaks is Rowan's destiny, but he stepped back from it a long time ago. Hunting Kudlaks is Clay's mission, and he won't let anyone or anything take him away from it.

Rowan is hurt and stubborn, while Clay has been adrift for a long time. They both need someone to love and care for, but will they be able to admit it? Or will one of them stubbornly cling to their loneliness and lose the greatest love they can ever have?

Rowan
Copyright © 2023 Catherine Lievens
ISBN: 978-1-4874-3917-0
Cover art by Angela Waters

Published by eXtasy Books Inc

Look for us online at:
www.eXtasybooks.com

Rowan
Krsnik Clan 1

By

Catherine Lievens

CHAPTER ONE

Rowan scrubbed the counter to give himself something to do, then glanced around the bar. The few people hanging around all had a drink, which meant that, at the moment, Rowan didn't have anything to do.

He hated when that happened.

He was always better when he could stay busy and avoid his mind wandering. Bad things happened when he allowed his mind to go where it wanted, and since he was at work, he'd rather not end up curled up in a corner crying for his dead family.

So instead, he started cleaning the counter again.

"You should take your break," Crystal said as she placed her tray on the counter and slid it toward him.

Grateful for something to do, he grabbed it, took the dirty glasses off it, rinsed them in the sink, then placed them into the dishwasher. "I'm fine," he grumbled.

Crystal arched a blonde brow. "Are you?"

She never believed him, and she was right not to. Rowan was a liar, and he had been all his life. Since he was a kid, he'd told himself everything would be okay.

That was the biggest lie he'd ever told himself.

Rowan forced himself to smile. "I'm fine," he repeated. "It's not like there's a lot of work to do."

"Which is why you should take your break. Lacey and I will be fine. Besides, it's not like you're going far."

She wouldn't let it go until Rowan agreed, so he glanced up again. He wouldn't leave Crystal and Lacey alone in the room if he thought any of the people sitting there were a danger to them. He could only see regulars, though, and besides, Tommy was at the door, keeping an eye on things. The girls would be okay, even if Rowan left them on their own to deal with the customers for half an hour.

Rowan sighed heavily and glared a little at Crystal. She didn't seem to care — she just stared until he finished cleaning the tray and handed it back to her. "I'm taking my break," Rowan grumbled, drying his hands.

"Good. And if you happen to go to that sandwich shop, bring back something, all right?"

Rowan hadn't planned on going, but he would now that Crystal had mentioned it. He didn't have to ask what she wanted because, like everyone else, she had a standing order.

He tugged off his apron and left it behind the bar before heading to the back room, where he'd left his backpack and jacket. He'd need his wallet if he was going to do this. He hadn't planned on getting dinner, but he suspected Crystal would find out if he didn't, and she'd let him know what she thought of him not eating.

He wasn't sure when any of this had happened, but he seemed to have found a family. It was nothing like the family he'd lost, but it still warmed his heart to have people who cared about him. Crystal would have gotten worried if he'd insisted that he didn't have to take a break. She wanted him to be happy, and while he doubted that was in the cards for him given his past, he could be at least content.

He was. His life was fine, and that was perfect as long as he didn't have expectations. He had a normal apartment. It wasn't extraordinary, but it also wasn't too bad. He liked his job, even though it didn't pay much.

And that was that. That was Rowan's entire life, nothing more, nothing less.

He left the bar and headed to the sandwich shop, putting

in the usual bar order. Tommy had been thinking about opening up the kitchen to get at least a few bar foods going, but he'd need to renovate the kitchen, and of course, he'd have to apply for licenses and whatnot. Rowan was glad he wasn't the owner. He didn't understand half of what Tommy regularly grumbled about when it came to taxes and all of that. Still, it would be nice not to have to leave the bar to get food, especially in the winter.

Thankfully, it was almost summer now, and the weather was nice. The air was warm, even this late at night, and it was nice to smell the night air rather than the air inside the bar. That was all beer and sweat, which wasn't exactly pleasant to Rowan's shifter nose.

He was less grumpy by the time he got back to the bar, maybe because his stomach was full. He had several bags in his hands, and as soon as he stepped in, he lifted them so everyone could see them. Lacey squeaked, then rushed toward him, making grabby hands. He wasn't sure what was in which bag, so he handed everything over to her.

"I'm starving," she said, leaning closer to kiss his cheek. "Thank you so much."

"Don't worry about it, and eat while it's still warm."

"Are you eating with us or getting back behind the bar?"

"I'm back at work. I already ate so there'd be someone to take care of the customers."

She nodded and walked toward the corner of the room where she and the others usually gathered. In most bars, the owners wouldn't have allowed servers or bartenders to eat during their shift, but Tommy was relaxed. The customers were used to seeing it, and no one had anything to say as long as there was someone behind the bar to pour drinks.

Which was where Rowan came in.

He grinned as Tommy left his stool to go stand with Lacey so he could see what was in the bags. Rowan had thought of him, too, and Tommy gave him a thumbs up when he saw that was the case.

"Hi," a woman said, getting Rowan's attention.

He smiled at her. "What can I get you?"

She leaned forward, her arms bracketing her breasts. Rowan had been at this job long enough to see what she was doing. The position was meant for him to get a good look at her chest, and he would have enjoyed it if he hadn't been gay.

The woman was pretty, with bright red lipstick and warm brown hair. She wore a pair of tight jeans and a tank top, and there was no doubt in Rowan's mind as to what she wanted. Unfortunately for her, she wasn't going to get it, at least not from him.

"A beer," she purred.

Rowan nodded, staying professional. "I'll be right with you."

He went to work, getting her beer ready, then handing it to her. She pouted a bit when she realized he wouldn't give her what she wanted, but thankfully, she could take no for an answer.

Women usually did. It was often the guys who were a problem, and Rowan looked around again to ensure everyone was behaving the way they should. As he did so, his gaze snagged on a guy sitting close to the door. He had his back to the wall as he looked around the room, his gaze moving from one table to another.

Then his gaze stopped on Rowan.

They stared at each other. The guy had to be in his mid-twenties, and if Rowan had to guess, he'd say the guy was human. He didn't have any of the vibes shifters or other supernatural creatures usually had, but that didn't mean he wasn't dangerous.

He didn't look like it, even though he had a curious vibe that made Rowan's sense of danger sit up. He didn't expect the guy to start attacking people, but there had to be a reason the human was watching him. It might only be for the same reason the woman who'd ordered a beer had been watching Rowan, but Rowan believed he could never be too careful.

As he continued working, he kept an eye on the guy at the table. His shaggy brown hair fell in front of his eyes, and he had to push it away a few times. That haircut was a bad idea if the guy was a fighter, because it would give the person he fought with a hold on him, but it was none of Rowan's business, just like the man's broad shoulders weren't.

The guy wasn't cute, but he was handsome, and if Rowan hadn't been fine on his own, he'd definitely have bought the guy a drink. He looked up again only to notice movement at the back of the room. His eyes widened when he recognized a Kudlak at a table there.

What the fuck? Usually they didn't stick around when they recognized Rowan as a Krsnik, so why was this one still here? And what about the human?

Rowan had no answers, and he had no idea what to do. As it was, he stayed right where he was and focused on doing his job, even though his brain was stuck.

Who was that guy, and why was he here? More importantly, *what* was he?

Clay couldn't look away from the bartender. The man hadn't been there when Clay entered the bar, but he'd arrived soon after, and Clay had noticed him immediately. Now that he had, it was hard to focus on the reason he was here.

He forced himself to look away from the guy behind the bar and toward the guy he'd followed here. The Kudlak was at a table at the back of the room, almost hidden in darkness. One of the waitresses had brought him a beer, but as far as Clay could see, he hadn't even taken a sip. Clay hadn't expected him to, but he'd thought this Kudlak would be smarter. Someone was bound to notice if he was the only one not drinking in the bar.

Clay had his own beer in front of him, and even though he needed to keep his wits, he took a sip. He wouldn't drink enough to get drunk because he had work to do, but at least he was better at mingling with people. The Kudlak didn't seem to care about mingling and kept staring at one of the waitresses. The way he looked at her made the hair on the back of Clay's neck rise, and he knew he'd done the right thing by coming here tonight.

He'd been following the Kudlak for several nights and planned to attack the monster tonight. He wanted answers, and he knew many ways to get them. Then, once he was finished with the Kudlak, he'd kill him.

But he'd have to catch him first. That was never easy, especially because Clay was human. The Kudlak was anything but, and most humans wouldn't even try to stop him.

It was lucky that Clay wasn't most humans.

But first, he'd need to see what the Kudlak decided to do.

He was careful not to stare too much at the Kudlak, which meant he had to allow his gaze to wander around the room while he drank as little as possible. Before, he'd been watching everyone in the room aimlessly. Now, every time he looked away from the Kudlak, his gaze went straight to the bartender.

Okay, so the man was hot. His hair was so dark it looked almost black, and maybe it was. Clay couldn't tell because it was dark in the bar, but he'd be game to find out. He'd also be game to find out what the man's lithe body felt like under his touch.

The bartender was dressed entirely in black—black jeans molded to his skin, black boots, and a black t-shirt. His skin was pale, which made an interesting aesthetic. Clay wasn't usually into emo guys, but he'd make an exception for this one.

As soon as he'd dispatched the Kudlak, anyway.

He peeked at the Kudlak again, but the monster was still sitting at his table, not even trying to behave like a human. It was a miracle no one around the room had noticed him, although as soon as Clay thought that, he realized that wasn't true. The bartender was staring at the Kudlak, his expression hard and almost angry. Did he know what the Kudlak was? Or did he, like most people in the room, only see him as human?

There could be nothing further from the truth, because Kudlaks weren't humans. They hunted humans and ate them.

The thought made Clay think about his family, and he had to look away, even for just one moment. He was here to get answers, and he'd get them. He'd find out who had killed his family, then he'd hunt and kill them just like they'd hunted and killed the people he loved.

The Kudlak had looked away from the waitress and fixated on another woman. She was here with a guy, and Clay was keeping an eye on her, not just because of the Kudlak. The guy with her looked at her like he wanted to eat her, and while she seemed okay with that at the moment, she'd been drinking a bit.

But what happened with that guy was none of Clay's business. His only focus was the Kudlak, so after the Kudlak got up to follow the couple out of the bar, Clay did the same. He couldn't allow the Kudlak to get too far, but he still gave the monster a few minutes to get ahead Then, he rushed out of his seat and toward the door.

He couldn't resist glancing back one last time before opening the door. The bartender was staring at him with wide eyes, and Clay winked at him, hoping he'd find him still there when he was done with the Kudlak. Maybe his evening wouldn't be so bad after all.

But first, Clay had work to do.

He left the bar and paused, looking around. He could hear the woman giggling from somewhere at the back of the parking lot, so that was where he headed. He didn't look around for the woman but for the Kudlak. They were great at hiding in the darkness because they were nocturnal. They hunted during the night when humans were at their most vulnerable.

That was where Clay came in. He wasn't a superhero and had never claimed to be one, but he protected people. He hadn't been able to protect his family, and while he knew that wasn't his fault, he'd been trying to fix it since they'd died.

The sound of someone falling, then a screech, told Clay that the Kudlak had found his victim. There was no need for Clay to hide anymore, so he ran ahead, his hand going to his waist. He took out his gun with the tranquilizers, ready to kick the Kudlak's ass.

He ran around the car, almost stumbling on someone stretched out on the ground. It was the man the woman had been drinking with, and she wasn't far off. She was leaning as far away from the Kudlak as possible, almost climbing the car she was trapped against. The Kudlak looked smug, but that wouldn't last long if Clay had anything to say about it.

"Hey," he said.

The Kudlak turned toward him. In the beginning, Clay had been terrified when he faced Kudlaks, but he'd gotten over it a while ago. Now, he just wanted to get to the point.

"Why don't you fight me?" he said, gesturing for the Kudlak to come closer. "I'll put up more of a fight."

The Kudlak growled, exposing his fangs. The woman screamed, but thankfully, the Kudlak was focused on Clay now. Clay wanted to tell her to run, but if she was smart, she'd figure it out without him having to prompt her. He couldn't look away from the Kudlak because if he did, he'd end up dead, and that wasn't how he wanted the evening to go.

The Kudlak was fast, but then, they all were. He slammed against Clay's body, pushing him back against one of the cars. Luckily, Clay had expected a full-on attack—that was how Kudlaks usually worked. He had a knife in his hand, his gun in the other. He raised his knife, feigning an attack while shooting the Kudlak in the stomach.

The Kudlak jerked back and looked down, appearing almost surprised at the fact that Clay had managed to shoot him. Clay grinned at him, ready to do so much more. Clay shot him a second time, but the Kudlak had been expecting it. He twisted out of the way, grabbed Clay's wrist, and dug his claws into it. It hurt, and Clay's first instinct was to let go of the gun. It clattered on the ground, and the Kudlak was smart enough to kick it away.

That left Clay with only his knife. He'd killed Kudlaks with much less, so he had faith he could do it, but it still unnerved him.

But he was here for a reason. He wanted answers, and he'd get them.

This time, they threw themselves at each other Clay trying to stab the Kudlak anywhere he could while keeping him alive and the Kudlak trying to bite Clay's neck. Clay could see the fangs poking under the Kudlak's lips as they moved. He'd felt them on his skin before, and it wasn't an experience he wanted to repeat. He wouldn't be food for this monster.

He'd be the monster's worst nightmare.

Or at least that was what he'd been planning until he stumbled over the guy on the ground. Why was he still there? No way would anyone have stayed through everything that had happened. Clay's stomach churned when he raised his hand and saw it was dirty with blood.

The Kudlak had killed the guy.

Claws grabbed Clay's wrist and hauled him up. He tried to

pull back, but the Kudlak wrapped his arms around Clay's body, pinning his arms to his sides. He could feel the Kudlak's breath on his neck, and his entire body went rigid.

He was about to die.

Rowan should have noticed the Kudlak much sooner than he had, but he'd been distracted by the handsome human at that table. He hadn't missed the fact that the human had left right after the Kudlak, who'd followed a couple out the door.

Was the hunter being hunted? It was entirely possible, but if so, there was no way the human would come out of it victorious. Rowan had met his fair share of Kudlaks, and humans seldom could fight them without getting hurt—or worse. A part of him wanted to let the human deal with all of this because it was none of his business, yet at the same time, it *felt* like his business.

His mother would have been appalled if he didn't help. The human might be a fool, but he'd seen what Rowan had seen. They both knew the Kudlak would attack the couple, and the human clearly was going to try to stop him.

Rowan quickly looked around. He waved Crystal closer, then gestured at the back door. "I left something in my car. I'll be right back."

She blinked, clearly surprised because he wasn't one to leave work, but she didn't try to stop him. She knew he wouldn't be leaving if it wasn't important.

And it was. Rowan hadn't fought a Kudlak in a long time, but he might be about to in order to save three lives.

He stopped at his backpack, quickly retrieving his two knives. Then he left through the back door.

If he were a Kudlak, the parking lot was where he'd attack, so he ran in that direction. He could hear the sounds of a scuffle, but when the sounds stopped, he knew he didn't have much time.

He ran faster, looking around until his gaze stopped on a pair of people embracing. The parking lot was dark, but not too dark for Rowan to see that one of the people in the embrace was the guy who'd been inside.

The other was the Kudlak.

Rowan prayed he was in time as he grabbed the Kudlak's shirt and pulled him back. The Kudlak hadn't expected him, and he let go of the human more quickly than Rowan had thought he would. He turned to Rowan, hissing and showing him his fangs.

Rowan did the same.

He wasn't scared of the Kudlak. He wasn't intimidated or cowed. He wanted the Kudlak to die, and he grinned as he raised his knives.

The Kudlak screeched and launched himself at Rowan. Rowan was rusty and hadn't done this in a long time, but he danced out of the way, his body remembering how to do it. It was exhilarating, and for a moment, it felt as if everything was back to the way it had been before.

But this wasn't Rowan's life anymore. He'd never taken pleasure in killing, and he wouldn't this time, either. He wanted this to be over as soon as possible so that no one would notice what was happening in the parking lot, so he focused on dispatching the Kudlak. This one had been attacking a human, and he deserved to die. More than deserved, it was necessary, because the Kudlaks who took human lives never stopped.

The Kudlak fought with his claws, so Rowan had the advantage. It wouldn't last long if the Kudlak decided to shift, so Rowan hoped it wouldn't. He didn't have a change of clothes with him, and it would be awkward to go back into the bar and have to explain what had happened and about his past. He was pretty sure Crystal knew he wasn't human, but she'd never asked, and he hadn't volunteered any information.

He wasn't planning to do so anytime soon.

Luckily, this Kudlak was young. He'd managed to pin down the human without too many problems, but Rowan wasn't human. He was faster and stronger, and he'd been trained to do this. It was in his blood, and his body hadn't forgotten how to do it.

He punched the Kudlak on the nose, smiling at the satisfying crunch. When the Kudlak cried out and folded in half, reaching for his nose, Rowan hit him on the back of the head. The Kudlak went down, curled into a ball, but it didn't take long for Rowan to find the heart and stab one of his knives right into it.

The Kudlak convulsed for a few seconds before going still. Rowan was out of breath, which was a sure sign he hadn't kept up with his training as well as he thought he had, but it had been enough for tonight.

He looked around. Kudlaks often hunted in pairs, but this one had been alone in the bar, and Rowan couldn't see other Kudlaks around. He leaned down to clean his knife on the Kudlak's shirt, then got ready to get back to work. The human the Kudlak had pinned earlier was still against the wall, but Rowan ignored him and hoped the human would do the same.

He should have known his luck wouldn't hold.

"What the fuck was that?" the human asked.

He grabbed Rowan's wrist as Rowan walked past him, and Rowan twirled around, slamming him against the wall.

It brought them close enough for Rowan to smell the human. There was sweat and fear, but more importantly, there was the scent of mate. Rowan jerked back, his eyes wide. This couldn't be.

"What the fuck was that?" the human asked, seemingly not

caring that Rowan had been pinning him against the wall seconds earlier.

"Are you okay?" Rowan found himself asking, even though he hadn't meant to. He'd already have left if this was a normal human, but it wasn't.

It was his mate.

This couldn't be possible. Krsniks had mates, just like every other shifter, but more often than not, they didn't live long enough to meet them. It was almost unheard of for them to meet their mates, and they'd never felt the same reverence and awe as other shifters had when it came to that. For there to be more Krsniks, they had to have children, and they didn't have the luxury of waiting to find their mate to do so, so they got married extremely young and had as many kids as possible.

Or at least, that was how things had gone before. By now, almost all of them were dead, and the few that were left didn't hunt anymore. Rowan certainly didn't and had no plans to start again.

The human looked up at Rowan. He was broader than Rowan and more muscled but shorter by several inches. That didn't seem to bother him as he leaned closer. "What the fuck was that?"

Rowan shook his head. "Nothing happened. You're safe."

The human snorted. "Because you killed that damn Kudlak. How did you know how to do that? Are you a hunter?"

Rowan's stomach dropped. He couldn't do this. He was nothing and didn't want that to change after everything he lost.

He took a step back, then another. It didn't matter that this man was his mate, because he had no intention of doing anything about it. He'd already lost too many people. He couldn't afford to start caring for another person, only for them to be taken away from him the way his family had.

"Where are you going?" the human asked, reaching for Rowan. "We need to talk about this because, man, it was incredible. Are you a professional? There's no way you're not, but why are you working in this bar if you are? We could work together."

Rowan ignored the many questions coming from his mate, turned around, and left.

Clay was so shocked that he couldn't do anything but watch the bartender walk away. The man had saved his life. Clay had no doubt that the Kudlak would have drunk him dry if the bartender hadn't stepped in and killed the monster.

Clay glanced down at the body on the ground. He'd been planning to interrogate the Kudlak before killing him, and he was dismayed that he wouldn't be able to do so, but this was fine. He'd rather be unable to interrogate the Kudlak than be dead.

But he wanted to know about the bartender. The man had been fierce and incredibly hot as he'd fought the Kudlak, and it was clear he knew what he was doing. There was no way he wasn't a hunter, but for some reason, he hadn't wanted Clay to know. Maybe he thought Clay was just another human. Clay supposed he was, but he was also a hunter, and while he wasn't happy about it, he had to admit he might need help.

He looked around the parking lot, but the woman from before seemed to have vanished. He had no doubt she was calling the police, so he quickly rushed after the bartender after picking up his gun. He couldn't do anything about the two bodies on the ground. The police would take care of them, and he'd be just another customer at the bar, having no idea what had happened.

As long as the bartender went along with that story,

anyway.

"Wait up," Clay said as he reached the bartender. The man was almost at the bar's back door, and to Clay's relief, he paused.

"We need to talk," Clay said. "I'm Clay, by the way. Thank you for saving my life."

"What did you think you were doing?" The bartender asked. He sounded angry, which didn't make sense.

"I was hunting. I'm a hunter."

The bartender turned toward Clay.

Clay had no idea why he was so pissed, and he wasn't sure he wanted to find out.

"You're not a hunter. You're human, and humans weren't born to hunt Kudlaks."

Clay had no idea what that meant. "Someone has to do it. You were great out there, so maybe you can help."

"You need to leave," the bartender snapped.

"What's your name?" Clay was curious, and he didn't want this conversation to end.

The bartender didn't seem to know what to make of Clay. "Will you leave if I tell you?"

"I can't make that kind of promise," Clay said with a grin.

The bartender hesitated, then sighed. "I'm Rowan."

"Well, it's a pleasure to meet you, Rowan. As I said before, I'm Clay. Thank you for saving my ass."

"What did you think you were doing? You can't attack a Kudlak on your own like that."

"He was going to kill that woman. He killed the guy she was with."

Clay didn't think the way Rowan's expression tightened meant he was afraid. He seemed more annoyed, which was puzzling and made Clay want to ask why he felt that way.

"Dammit," Rowan muttered. "You think someone called the police?"

"Probably the woman after I saved her from the Kudlak. So, can we talk?"

Rowan shook his head and pushed open the back door. "You need to leave me alone."

"We have to talk about what just happened," Clay insisted.

Rowan tried to close the door, but Clay caught it. He started to step inside, but the guy who'd been at the front door earlier appeared at the end of the hallway.

He looked from Clay to Rowan, a frown appearing on his face. "Is everything okay here?"

"Clay was just leaving," Rowan said.

"I can wait for you if you have to go back to work," Clay insisted. For some reason, he felt like if he didn't, he'd lose any chance he might have with Rowan. It was ridiculous because he only wanted to talk to Rowan about his skills as a Kudlak hunter, but he needed more time.

Rowan shook his head and walked away, but when Clay started to follow, the bouncer shook his head. "You need to let him go." The man's voice was hard and told Clay he meant business. Clay could have fought him, but he doubted it was the best way to get Rowan to talk to him.

He raised his hands. "I'm sorry."

The bouncer nodded. "That's fine. You can't be here, though. It's the back door."

"All right."

Clay stepped back into the parking lot. He could hear sirens, which meant the police were coming. He was still tempted to walk around the bar and get in through the front door, but he doubted Rowan would talk to him tonight. Besides, the further away he was when the police arrived, the better it would be.

So instead of going back in like he wanted to, he turned and walked away. He hadn't parked in the parking lot, just in case, and he was glad he hadn't. He kept his pace normal so he wouldn't look suspicious, but he still reached his car before the police got to the parking lot. He slid into the driver seat and closed the door, but he didn't turn the engine on right away. He kept replaying the short fight between the Kudlak and Rowan. Rowan had been impressive, and not just because he clearly knew what he was doing.

Rowan wasn't the kind of guy Clay usually went for. He hadn't seemed interested, but maybe that was because he'd been trying to run from Clay. Clay didn't know why, but he intended to find out. When he wanted something, he usually got it, and while he wasn't about to force Rowan into anything he didn't want, he hoped to get some answers.

Clay had worked with hunters before, but none of them had been like Rowan. There was more to him than met the eye, and Clay wanted to find out what that more was. It was clear Rowan wouldn't make it easy for him, but that wouldn't be enough to deter him.

But Clay wouldn't be able to do anything tonight, so he finally started his car and headed home. He stopped on the way to get pizza, but even by the time he got home, he wasn't able to stop thinking about Rowan. The shitty apartment he was staying in at the moment didn't have any distractions, so as he ate, he allowed his mind to focus on Rowan.

Why was he working as a bartender? Was it a way for him to keep an eye on the Kudlaks? Bars were good hunting ground for them, so it would make sense. But if so, why hadn't Rowan agreed to talk to Clay? He'd almost run away after killing the Kudlak, and Clay didn't understand why. He'd also looked angry, which made even less sense.

Clay sighed and leaned back against the couch. He wished he could call his mother. They could have talked this out, and she no doubt would have had good advice for him. He couldn't call, though. She was nothing more than a memory, all because of a Kudlak.

One day, Clay would find the Kudlak who'd killed his family, and he'd make them pay. Hopefully, he'd have someone as strong and skilled as Rowan when that happened. Not having anyone wouldn't stop him, though. There was a reason he'd become a hunter, and he wouldn't stop until he got his hands on the Kudlak who'd hurt him so badly and had taken everything from him.

That was why Clay needed to convince Rowan to help him. With him by his side, he could get his revenge.

And that was all that mattered.

Chapter Two

Rowan didn't know what to do. Even though he didn't want to lose anyone else in his life, Clay was his mate. It was important, and Rowan couldn't just ignore the fact that he'd met him.

He kept thinking of Clay throughout his day, grocery shopping and getting ready for work. It would be better to stay away from Clay. There was no way to know what Clay would think about being Rowan's mate, even though he must have known about Krsniks. Maybe he didn't know about them and only knew about Kudlaks. Rowan should probably have asked yesterday evening, but he'd been overwhelmed and had needed to get away from the parking lot.

And he'd been right to do so. He'd been back at work, acting as if everything was okay, when the police had come to the bar. They wanted to know if anyone had heard anything, but Rowan hadn't stepped up, even though Crystal had been staring at him. Thankfully, she hadn't said anything about the fact that he'd been in the parking lot getting something from his car when the man and the Kudlak had been killed. She and the others knew there was something in Rowan's past, but they'd never asked for details, and he doubted they ever would. They seemed to be able to feel that he wasn't quite human, though, and that was fine with him. He didn't want to hide the fact that he wasn't human. He just didn't want anything to do with Kudlaks and hunters.

But it wasn't that easy. He didn't know if Clay was a hunter or if his presence in the parking lot last night had been a coincidence. Maybe he'd been leaving and had noticed something was wrong.

That didn't feel right. He'd followed the Kudlak out of the bar, just like Rowan had followed him. That meant Clay knew what Kudlaks were and what this one had been planning. He could have stopped the couple from leaving, but instead, he'd allowed the man to be killed.

Rowan shook his head. He couldn't think like that. He knew how difficult it was to hunt Kudlaks, and he was sure Clay had done everything he could. The fact remained that if he was a hunter, Rowan couldn't afford to let him in. His heart wouldn't survive if he had to lose someone else, especially to the Kudlaks. As far as he was concerned, he was better off on his own than with someone who could die at any moment because of what they did for a living.

Rowan realized in his car that all of this might be pointless. He didn't have Clay's number, and Clay didn't have his. Clay might never come back to the bar, and Rowan told himself that would be for the best. He should be happy that he'd probably never see Clay again.

But he couldn't be.

He thumped his forehead against the steering wheel before starting the car. Whatever happened, he'd deal with it. He always did, and this situation wouldn't be any different. Would he rather have met Clay in different circumstances? Of course. He wished he could have a chance with his mate, but he needed to protect himself. He'd lost enough over the decades. He couldn't lose anyone else, especially not his mate. He couldn't afford for their bond to strengthen only to have it cut. That meant that if Clay returned to the bar, Rowan would have to shut him out.

He was planning to do just that. He just wasn't sure if he could manage because Clay was his mate, not just a guy.

Rowan knew what he'd do if he were in Clay's place. Clay

was human, which meant he didn't know they were mates, but that didn't mean he couldn't feel the bond. If he did feel something, he'd come back tonight or maybe tomorrow. He'd been fine when he'd left last night, and hopefully, after his encounter with the Kudlak, he'd had the common sense to head home rather than sticking around and trying to kill other Kudlaks. They weren't easily found, but something told Rowan that this hadn't been a fluke. Clay had probably been following the Kudlak for several days, but unless the Kudlak had come into the bar when Rowan wasn't there, last night had been the first time he was there. Rowan prided himself on keeping his coworkers safe, which meant that every evening, he walked Lacey and Crystal to their cars. He made sure they got out of the parking lot safely, and only then did he head home. It would have been the perfect moment for a Kudlak to attack, but instead, the Kudlak had waited until last night, which told Rowan it was the first time he'd been there.

That was a good thing. It meant Rowan wasn't entirely losing his touch, although he wouldn't have minded if he had been. The hunter's life wasn't his anymore, and he didn't want it back, which was something else he was afraid of. He'd seen how excited Clay had been last night, and he suspected Clay would ask him to join him when he came back. His answer could only be no, but he didn't know how Clay would take it.

He parked in the lot behind the bar, but instead of going inside right away, he poked around for a bit. There would be no way for him to know if someone snuck in while he was at work, but everything was as it should be for now. There was no Kudlak in sight, and Rowan hoped it would stay that way.

The start of the evening went like every other day. He got to the bar, did a brief inventory, and got ready to work. Everyone else was there, and when the bar opened, the first customers started streaming in. Rowan focused on the work, but there was always a lull after a while, and that was when Clay found him.

Rowan looked up to find Clay coming toward him. His mate was staring at him, which meant Rowan couldn't escape. So he forced himself to stay where he was and acted as if he didn't care that Clay was there. In reality, his heart was beating out of his chest, almost as if it was trying to get to Clay.

"Hi," Clay said as he hopped onto a stool.

Rowan nodded at him. "What can I get you?"

Clay leaned forward. "How about your phone number?"

Rowan grimaced. "That wasn't exactly smooth."

Thankfully, it made Clay laugh. "I wasn't trying to be. I just want to be able to call you instead of coming around the bar every time I need to talk to you."

Rowan crossed his arms over his chest. "Why would you need to talk to me?"

"Because of what happened last night. We could work together."

Rowan shook his head. "I'm a bartender. So what do you want to drink?"

"Is there a problem here?" Tommy asked, looking from Clay to Rowan.

Clay grinned at him, but Rowan clearly had been distracted if he hadn't noticed a human coming closer. It was all Clay's fault, or maybe it was Rowan's for allowing Clay to do it. Rowan wanted to continue talking to him, even though it would be best if he didn't. He didn't want Clay to get kicked out, yet at the same time, he couldn't give him what he wanted.

"Everything's fine," he reassured his boss.

Tommy didn't look convinced. "You're sure? I remember this guy from last night."

Rowan knew what Tommy wasn't saying. He remembered

this guy had been in the parking lot, and two bodies had been found there. The police had concluded that the Kudlak had killed the man, but they had no idea who had killed the Kudlak.

"He's a friend," Rowan reassured Tommy. "He's just here to tell me something, but he's leaving."

"I am?" Clay asked, sounding surprised.

He'd clearly expected Rowan to welcome him with open arms, but Rowan couldn't do that. Clay couldn't understand — or maybe he could. They were only a few reasons for humans to hunt Kudlaks, and revenge was one of them.

But even though Kudlaks had killed Rowan's family, he didn't want revenge. He wanted to be left alone, far away from that world, and he didn't know if Clay would understand that. Humans were especially bloodthirsty when it came to revenge.

Tommy didn't look convinced, but he nodded and headed back toward his stool.

"I'm not leaving," Clay said, leaning forward.

"You can stay, but you're not going to get what you want from me," Rowan told him, staring right at him. He didn't want to intimidate his mate, but he would if that was what he needed to do to get Clay to leave him alone.

Clay had no idea what was happening, but he was relieved the bouncer wasn't kicking him out. It gave him an opportunity to convince Rowan to talk to him, which was all he needed, at least for now.

"Well, you're not wrong. I do need to tell you something," he told Rowan. "I'll have a beer."

Rowan looked like he wanted to throw the beer in his face rather than let him drink it, but he didn't. Instead, he filled a glass, placed it in front of Clay, and waited for Clay to pay.

As soon as Clay had, Rowan turned to leave.

Clay wouldn't let him go that easily.

He caught Clay's wrist and pulled him close. He peeked back just in case the bouncer had decided to come back, but he was watching the door and talking to a woman. That meant Clay had a few minutes—unless Rowan kicked his ass, which considering last night, was entirely possible.

"Let me go," Rowan snapped, looking around as he did so. He clearly didn't want the people around them to realize how uncomfortable he was, and it was working, because no one looked their way.

But Clay let him go anyway. He didn't want to make Rowan uncomfortable. He just wanted a chance to talk to him.

"I'm sorry about that." Clay kept touching him, and he wasn't usually a touchy-feely kind of guy. Something in him just wanted to be close to Rowan.

"You need to leave me alone," Rowan said. "I have nothing to give you."

"You're a hunter." Or he had been once. He'd known what to do with the Kudlak last night, but he didn't seem to be hunting regularly right now. Maybe the bar was his hunting ground, but Clay hadn't seen any other Kudlaks in the time he'd spent here, so he doubted that was the case.

"And you're going to get yourself killed. You don't know what you're doing. Kudlaks are dangerous, and no human can last long while hunting them."

"Well, I've been hunting them for a while, and I'm still here. You are, too."

Rowan grinned, and Clay jerked backward when he saw fangs in his mouth. Was he a Kudlak? That didn't make sense, and Clay didn't feel the same danger when he was close to Rowan. He had plenty of other feelings, but not that one.

"I'm still here because I was born to hunt Kudlaks," Rowan said slowly. "You weren't. You're human, and eventually, you'll get yourself killed. It's not my business, but I have no intention of losing someone else, so leave me alone."

Clay sucked in a breath. If Rowan had been born to kill them, he had to be a Krsnik.

Clay had always thought they were a legend. He'd never met a Krsnik and hadn't thought he would. The few hunters he'd met who knew about Krsniks had told him they were all gone, killed in the fights with the Kudlaks. Was Rowan the last one standing? And if so, why wasn't he fighting the Kudlaks and getting revenge for what they'd done to his people?

Rowan waved at the bouncer, but Clay didn't try to stop him. He wouldn't get anything else as long as they were in the bar. They needed to be able to talk freely, and that wasn't going to happen here, so he got to his feet. "I'll go," he told Rowan.

Rowan stared at him. "But you'll come back."

Clay grinned. "How can I not? You're a Krsnik. Do you know how rare you guys are?"

"I know how many of us there were. I also know how many of us died."

Clay's smile faded, and he stepped away from the counter. So he was right. Rowan had lost his people, which probably was why he'd stopped hunting Kudlaks.

The bouncer reached Clay as Clay walked away. He wanted to stay and continue talking to Rowan, but this was all he'd get at the moment.

He wasn't done, and he was pretty sure Rowan was aware of that.

Instead of going home, Clay walked around the bar and headed to the parking lot. He doubted any Kudlak would come around considering what had happened last night, but he still kept his eyes open. His gaze flickered to the area where the Kudlak had killed that guy and had then been killed by Rowan. It was taped off with yellow police tape, and

25

everyone had given it a wide berth and parked their cars on the other side of the lot. Clay wasn't planning to go anywhere close to that area, so instead, he leaned against the wall, close enough to the back door to be able to see it when it opened.

Then he waited.

He'd never had much patience as a kid, but he'd learned it after becoming a hunter. He couldn't afford to be rash and possibly lose his prey when he hunted, which meant being quiet and still. It wasn't his favorite part of the hunt, but it was what he had to do, so he did it, even though Rowan wasn't a Kudlak.

It still felt like Clay was hunting him. Clay didn't understand why he felt like he might die if he didn't talk to Rowan. He was drawn to him in a way he'd never felt drawn to anyone, and it wasn't just because Rowan was incredibly sexy. There was something more to him.

Clay wanted to hold Rowan's hand and listen to him tell stories about his family. He wanted to hear Rowan's stories about the hunts and the Kudlaks he'd killed. He wanted to wrap him in his arms and keep him safe, and at the same time, he wanted them to hunt together.

It wouldn't be the first time Clay had hunted with someone else, but he could tell it would be the most interesting time. The other hunters he'd spent time with had been humans, but Rowan wasn't. He'd been born to hunt Kudlaks, and it had been incredible to watch yesterday.

Clay wanted to see it again.

He waited long hours, watching customers come in and out of the bar. Eventually, fewer of them arrived, then none. Silence descended on the parking lot, but still, Clay waited. He was getting cold, and his legs felt stiff, so he was glad when the back door opened.

A woman came out. Clay recognized her as one of the waitresses, so he didn't move toward her like he'd been planning if it had been Rowan. She still noticed him, and she squeaked as she started to step back into the bar. Someone came up behind her, and Clay recognized Rowan's voice.

"What is it?" Rowan asked.

"There's a guy in the parking lot."

The waitress stepped aside, and Rowan appeared. His gaze stopped on Clay, and he scowled. Clay expected to be snapped at, but Rowan turned his attention back to the waitress. "He's fine. He's waiting for me."

The waitress didn't seem convinced. "Are you sure? I can call Tommy."

"I'm sure. Let me walk you to your car."

Clay watched as Rowan walked both waitresses to their cars, then waited until they'd driven away. It looked like something they often did, maybe every evening. He clearly cared about them and didn't want anything to happen to them.

So why was he allowing Kudlaks to come to the bar?

"We need to talk," Clay declared as soon as Rowan was close enough.

"We don't need to do anything," Rowan snapped. "Stop coming here. I don't want to see you or to talk to you."

For some reason, Rowan appeared pained when he said those words. Maybe he did want to see Clay again but wasn't ready to admit it. Clay could, at least to himself. He wanted to see if there could be something between him and Rowan, but that wasn't the most important thing here. The most important thing was to hunt, and Clay needed Rowan's help.

"You can't waste your talent, and besides, you were born to hunt them," Clay said, moving closer as Rowan turned toward one of the last two cars in the lot.

"You won't convince me, so let it go," Rowan said, not looking up at Clay.

Clay grabbed his shoulder to turn him around, but Rowan

moved fast, and the only thing that saved Clay was his instincts. He raised his hands and crossed his forearms, stopping Rowan's punch with his body.

But Rowan wasn't done.

Rowan hadn't meant to attack Clay. He just wanted Clay to leave him alone, and when Clay had insisted, he'd gotten angry. That was the only explanation he could come up with to explain why he'd tried to punch his mate, but thankfully, Clay had stopped the punch.

But Rowan had started this. He wanted to pummel Clay into the ground and force him to listen. He wanted Clay to leave him alone and never come back.

He wanted to kiss Clay and claim him.

Instead, he threw another punch at Clay's face. Clay moved fast, which was a sure sign that he knew what he was doing, but he was still human. He might think it didn't mean much, but he couldn't have been more wrong, and Rowan had every intention of showing him just how unprepared he was to deal with Kudlaks. Krsniks were the Kudlaks' counterparts. They hunted Kudlaks and kept humanity safe, and they were equipped to do so. Even then, so many of his family had been killed that only Rowan was left. How could Clay not see how dangerous hunting Kudlaks was? Why didn't he care about his safety?

Clay didn't manage to block every punch Rowan aimed his way, and soon, he was bleeding from a cut on his lower lip. Rowan almost stopped, but Clay was grinning like an idiot. Either he was having fun, or he wasn't taking Rowan seriously, which was all Rowan wanted.

Even though Clay was his mate, Rowan knew better than to hope there could be anything between them. He needed to get Clay out of his life, and that wouldn't happen if he was gentle about it.

So he continued fighting. He punched at Clay's body, kicked at him, but tried to keep his hits from being too powerful. He could be lethal, and he wasn't about to kill Clay.

"You know, there are more pleasant ways to do this," Clay said as he caught one of Rowan's fists.

He squeezed his hand around it, and Rowan took the opportunity to crouch and kick at Clay's legs. Clay squeaked and finally went down. Rowan wouldn't allow him to get back up, so he quickly straddled him, caught his hands, and pinned them above his head. Clay was still smiling like an idiot as he bucked up his hips, and Rowan understood why when he felt the hard cock in Clay's jeans.

The fucker was aroused.

Well, that made Rowan a fucker, too, because he felt he might be about to come in his pants. It wasn't the fight per se, but rather having fought with his mate. His entire body yearned to have Clay's hands on him, and fighting had been a way to obtain that.

Clay grinned up at Rowan. In the light coming from the lamp above the door, Rowan could see blood dripping from the corner of Clay's lip. Before he could think better of it, he leaned down and licked it.

A shudder raked through his body. It had been so long since he'd drunk blood, and he knew he shouldn't have done that. Now, his body would want more of it—more of *Clay's* blood. His animal side wanted them to bite Clay and make him theirs, but Rowan knew better, so he leaned back.

"Have you had enough?" Rowan asked in a hard voice.

But Clay was still smiling. "It was great. Why are you a bartender when you can do this? You could kill so many Kudlaks and keep the world safe, but instead, you're hiding. What happened to you? Why don't you want to rid the world of Kudlaks?"

Rowan resisted the urge to punch Clay again and pushed away. He got to his feet, putting as much space between them as he could. "You humans only ever want one thing. You want blood, and you don't care what other people feel. Why are you so bent on hunting Kudlaks? Did they kill your family? Well, newsflash—you're not the only one. I'm done with hunting, and I'm never coming back. You need to leave me alone."

Clay sat up. "I don't have a choice." He didn't sound as happy as he had a few moments ago.

"Everyone has a choice, including you. What are you gaining from doing this?"

"What are you gaining from ignoring it? The Kudlaks are out there, killing people like they killed your family and mine. How can you not want to fight for that to end?"

Rowan didn't want to listen to Clay. He'd told himself everything Clay was saying time and time again, but he'd had enough. He'd been taught how to fight since he was a child. He'd been fighting since he was nothing more than a teenager, and the only things it had ever brought him were pain and death. Maybe it was his duty to continue hunting the Kudlaks, and maybe he was failing that duty and shaming his parents and his entire family who'd died for the cause, but he didn't care. He'd needed to stop before he lost himself, and he had. Nothing would bring his family back, and he was alone, but at least he was alive, and if he ever managed to build himself a family, he wouldn't lose them to the Kudlaks. That was all he cared about, but he wasn't sure Clay would understand or even if he could.

Clay got to his feet. Rowan steeled himself, expecting him to attack, but instead, he just stood there, poking at his lower lip and grimacing at the pain.

"You got me good."

"I told you to leave me alone."

"You did, and I should have. I'm sorry to hear what happened to your family, but you're not the only one who lost everything to the Kudlaks. Do you know how common it is to hear this kind of story within the hunters' community?"

Rowan snorted. "Hunters' community?"

"After you guys disappeared, someone had to step in to kill the Kudlaks. We might only be humans, but we do what we can. We thought you'd all died."

They were still a few Krsniks here and there, including Rowan. He'd met some of them, but none had been part of his village. They were strangers, even though they were Krsniks.

"You need to help us," Clay said, stepping closer but not close enough for Rowan to be able to catch him. "We need someone like you. *I* need someone like you by my side, helping me kill the Kudlaks. We can keep each other safe. I'm not promising it means we'll both make it out in one piece, but this is what you were born to do. You told me that yesterday."

"I'm not going to watch my mate get killed just because he's a stubborn asshole," Rowan yelled. "I lost too many people already. I'm not losing you, too. If you insist you want to hunt Kudlaks, then fine. Be my guest. But I won't stand there and watch you die."

Rowan was trembling. He'd said too much. He turned toward his car, but in a move Clay seemed to have perfected, he caught Rowan's wrist. Rowan froze and resisted the urge to snatch it away.

"Your mate?" Clay asked.

Because, of course, that was the only thing he'd listened to. He hadn't heard Rowan telling him it was dangerous to hunt Kudlaks, especially for humans. He hadn't heard Rowan telling him why he would never hunt Kudlaks again. He'd only heard what he wanted to hear, which was that he was Rowan's mate.

Rowan shook off Clay's hold and turned to face him. "It

doesn't change anything," he said through gritted teeth. "You're still a hunter, and I'm a bartender. I can't do this again."

But Clay was beaming. He reached for Rowan again, and Rowan steeled himself. He deserved to be punched after what he'd just done to Clay. Instead, Clay grabbed the back of Rowan's neck and pulled him close. Rowan realized this wasn't a fight when he smashed their lips together.

And for the first time in what felt like forever, he allowed himself to feel close to someone.

Clay had expected the fangs because he'd seen them earlier, but he hadn't thought Rowan's lips would be so soft.

Most of all, he hadn't thought Rowan would kiss him back.

But he was. As soon as their lips touched, Rowan pushed his way into Clay's arms. Clay stumbled back, but thankfully, the wall was there to hold them up. He turned until he could get Rowan's back against the wall, then pressed him against it, smiling when Rowan groaned.

He understood everything Rowan had been saying. He knew how much it hurt to lose his entire family to the Kudlaks and how it felt to want to die with them.

But he and Rowan were still there. They were alive, and they were kissing, and they were mates.

And Rowan's hands were on Clay's belt.

Clay tore his mouth away from Rowan's. He sucked in a breath, trying to put his thoughts into order, but that was impossible when Rowan's hand snaked into his jeans. Rowan's fingers clasped around Clay's hard cock, squeezing, and Clay thrust forward without meaning to.

Rowan had been driving him nuts before, but was nothing next to this. Clay had no idea what they were doing, but he cupped Rowan's cheek and kissed him again. At the same time, he used his other hand to find Rowan's cock in his jeans. He was hard, too, and after some wiggling and repositioning, Rowan managed to wrap his hand around both their cocks.

Clay enjoyed sex like everyone else, but he wasn't usually one to have it in the open. Thankfully, it was late, and no one was around. Even if someone were to walk down the street, they wouldn't see them unless they were looking for them. The light above the door illuminated them well enough that anyone who did stumble onto them would know what they were doing right away, but Clay didn't care.

He'd been shocked when Rowan yelled that he was his mate. That explained why he'd felt so drawn to Rowan, and it was good to know he wasn't going nuts. He didn't know what this would mean, but it didn't matter at the moment. It only meant that they were made for each other, and that was how Clay felt as Rowan stroked both of them.

He wanted more. He wanted *everything*, and for the first time, he could understand why Rowan wanted nothing to do with the Kudlaks and hunters in general. If Clay could have this for the rest of his life, maybe, it would be worth it.

Or maybe not. He wanted to keep people safe. He hadn't been able to do anything for his family, but he'd saved dozens of others over the years. Could he really give that up for Rowan? Could Rowan give up his retirement for Clay?

Clay forgot all about that as Rowan pushed both of them closer to the edge. Their kiss was intense now, and they panted into each other's mouths as if they'd just finished running a marathon. Clay was clinging to Rowan, trying to pull him closer even though there was no way to do it. They were already pressed together, and with the wall against Rowan's back, there was nowhere else for them to go.

Rowan nipped at Clay's lower lip with his fangs. He'd already tasted Clay's blood when he'd licked it from Clay's lips, but he didn't hesitate to suck the drop of blood that pearled in the spot where his fangs had broken the skin. It didn't hurt, although maybe that was because Clay was too focused on what Rowan was doing in his pants.

This had to be the most intense sexual experience Clay had ever had, and they were still wearing all their clothes. It felt like Rowan wanted to devour Clay, and Clay briefly wondered if, like Kudlaks, Krsniks drank blood. The fangs suggested that, but he couldn't find it in himself to care. Instead, when Rowan stopped sucking on his lip, he bit into it himself to give his mate more blood.

Rowan groaned and did what Clay wanted him to do. He sucked on Clay's lower lip, and between that and the sensation of Rowan's hand on his dick, Clay shuddered in pleasure. When he felt Rowan's cock twitch against his, it was all over. He came on Rowan's hand, getting both of them soiled, but it didn't matter because Rowan had done the same only seconds before.

Clay had no idea what had happened, but it felt like the world had shifted. Something inside of him had changed, and while he didn't know what it would mean in the future, right now, he never wanted to let go of Rowan. So he clung to him, keeping him close even when Rowan's body stiffened. Clay wasn't surprised that Rowan had already regretted what happened, but he didn't. If he had a choice, he'd do it again and again.

They were mates.

Clay might be human, but that didn't mean that having met his mate didn't mean anything to him. In fact, it meant a lot.

But it might not to Rowan, or it might not be enough.

When Rowan pushed Clay away, Clay stepped back. The night air was warm since it was June, but they were too exposed, so they both hurried to straighten their clothes. Clay was lucky since his hands were clean, but Rowan didn't seem to have a problem with it as he wiped his hand against the wall. Clay wrinkled his nose, then laughed.

"What are you laughing at?" Rowan asked.

"Just wondering what someone might think if they see the dirty spot," he said, gesturing at the wall.

Rowan looked away. For a moment, they were silent. Clay wanted to ask the many questions he had on his mind, but at the same time, it was nice to have a quiet moment with his mate.

Holy fuck. Even though he was human, he had a mate.

"So it's true?" he asked — he needed confirmation.

Rowan glared at him. "That you're my mate? It is."

Clay grinned and stepped closer. "It's perfect. We can hunt together, protect each other, and rid the world of Kudlaks."

Rowan looked pissed. Clay winced when Rowan punched the wall, but he understood. He'd just told himself not to push, yet only seconds later, he'd done so.

"Did you listen to anything I told you earlier?" Rowan said as he shook his hand. Drops of blood landed on the ground. "I don't want to be a hunter ever again. I've done my time and lost way more than anyone should lose. I'm done with that life. I'm done with all of it."

"Are you done with me, too?" Clay needed to know.

Rowan hesitated. "I don't want to be, but I'm not sure I have a choice. Are you willing to give up hunting?"

"I can't do that." And it wasn't because Clay had never thought about it. He had, usually after a fight, when he'd seen Kudlaks kill humans and when he was bleeding and sore. Sometimes, he wondered if it was worth the pain and loneliness.

Rowan sighed. "I need time. I didn't expect to meet my mate, and I certainly didn't expect him to be a Kudlak hunter. I don't know what I want or what I'll do."

Clay wanted nothing more than to drag Rowan into his

arms, but he didn't. Instead, he took a step back and raised his hands. "Go home. Sleep on it. Take your time, and I'll see you soon."

"You're going to come back tomorrow night, aren't you?"

Clay grinned. "How could I stay away when I know you're my mate?"

Clay truly felt that way. He hadn't expected to have a mate, and he certainly hadn't expected to be a Krsnik's mate, but this was what fate had chosen for him, and there had to be a reason for that. If Clay had needed to stop hunting, he wouldn't have been Rowan's mate. Fate was trying to tell both of them something, and hopefully, Rowan would see that.

CHAPTER THREE

Rowan wasn't at all surprised to see Clay at the bar the next evening. Hell, he would have been surprised *not* to see him, considering everything. Clay didn't strike Rowan as someone who took no for an answer, especially in the situation they were in. He wanted to talk, to try to convince Rowan to give him a chance or listen to him, even though nothing he could say would change Rowan's mind.

But Clay clearly didn't understand that. Whatever had happened to set him on the path he was on, he was bloodthirsty enough that he didn't care what could happen to him. He might understand how dangerous the Kudlaks were, but that wouldn't be enough to stop him from going after them.

Which meant that he and Rowan couldn't be together.

Yet, here he was, sitting on the other side of the counter, grinning at Rowan as if he was happy to see him. He probably was. Rowan wasn't sure whether he truly didn't understand what he'd been saying or if he'd just decided to ignore it. The fact that Rowan had admitted they were mates wasn't going to make the situation easier, and it already wasn't easy.

Trust fate to stick him with someone more stubborn than he was.

"What can I get you?"

"A conversation," Clay said before winking.

Rowan rolled his eyes—this was ridiculous. If Clay had gone straight to trying to convince Rowan to start hunting with him, it would have been easy for Rowan to tell him to fuck off. Instead, he was acting slightly goofy tonight, as if he wanted to try seducing Rowan. It was a massive change in behavior, one Rowan hadn't expected and wasn't sure how to deal with.

"To drink," he said, trying not to smile.

Clay beamed. "A beer is fine. Really, though. What do I have to do to have a conversation with you?"

"It seems we've been talking every evening for the past few days," Rowan pointed out as he got to work.

"Yeah, but it's not like we had any meaningful conversations. Mostly it's been us fighting, you beating me up, then fucking me against the wall."

Rowan sharply looked up, ready to scold Clay for saying that in public, but no one was listening to them, and Clay seemed to have known that. The smile was still firmly on his lips, and Rowan found himself relaxing even though he didn't mean to.

He couldn't afford to play nice. Clay needed to understand that Rowan was done with hunting and that whatever Clay wanted, that wasn't changing. Rowan had already told him that, though, and it didn't seem to matter, so he wasn't sure how to get Clay to let it go. He was starting to wonder if anything could.

He placed the beer in front of Clay. "There you go. I have work, though, so I can't talk."

"I can stay here until you're done working. I understand I can't be your priority right now." He made a show of looking around, and once again, Rowan had to resist the urge to slap him.

It didn't matter that it was a slow night and that Rowan could count the customers in the bar on the fingers of one hand. He was still at work, and that meant something to him.

"You're not as funny as you seem to think you are," he told Clay.

"Am I not?" His expression turned more serious. "But

really, I understand. You're at work, and you need to focus on that. I'm fine waiting here. I just wasn't sure how else to reach you, and I thought this would be easier than trying to corner you after work. I wouldn't want you to beat me up again."

Clay's lower lip was still slightly swollen, and a bruise had formed by his eye. The sight of the wounds made Rowan feel guilty. He'd been taught never to hurt someone who didn't deserve it, and no matter how frustrated he was with Clay, Clay hadn't deserved to be beaten. "I'm sorry for what I did to you."

"Don't be. It was fun."

"Only you could find me beating you up fun."

"I guess I can see why we're fated to be together."

Rowan swallowed. They should probably talk about that, but he wasn't sure what else there was to say. His entire being wanted to give Clay a chance. Clay was his opportunity to not be alone anymore, to finally have someone who would love him unconditionally and who wouldn't abandon him.

Except Clay might. It would be too easy for him to die at the hands of a Kudlak, and then Rowan would be back at square one, alone again and having lost the most important person in his life. He remembered all too well how much it hurt, and he'd never lost a mate. He wasn't sure he could survive if that happened.

Which meant he needed to keep Clay away.

That was easier said than done, because Clay was like a dog with a bone. Now that he knew Rowan was a Krsnik and his mate, he was eager to cling, and Rowan wasn't sure he'd have the strength to continue pushing him away. He was going to try, but so far, it hadn't worked. Rowan couldn't see how that would change, especially considering Clay's personality. He was stubborn, even more than Rowan, which was saying something.

Rowan went back to work, even though he had little to do.

A few more customers came in later in the night, but it wasn't enough to keep Rowan busy. Eventually, he drifted back to Clay, who was doing something on his phone. When he lowered it, Rowan saw it was that game with the candy. It made him want to roll his eyes again, but instead, he leaned over the counter and stared at Clay.

"Why are you here?"

Clay seemed to sense Rowan was being serious. "To talk to you," he said. There was still a hint of a smile on his lips, but his expression was serious. "You told me the Kudlaks killed your family. Well, they killed mine, too. They thought they killed me, but while I was wounded and unconscious, I survived." Clay's fingers drifted toward his neck. There were scars there, and Rowan recognized them all too easily. It made him want to hunt the Kudlaks who'd done this to his mate.

Clay lowered his hand to the counter and stared at it. "When I woke up, the house was on fire. I remember running through it, feeling weak and like I was about to die, looking for my family. I found them eventually, but it was too late. It had been too late for hours, but I hadn't known that. I tried to get them out, even though it was stupid because they were already dead. I almost lost my life a second time then, but the neighbors got me out. I don't remember much after that. I was in shock, and I'd lost a lot of blood. I didn't know what happened or what the Kudlaks were then, but eventually, I found out."

"And you decided to avenge your family."

Clay shrugged. "What else was I supposed to do? I didn't have anything else to live for. I still don't." His gaze flickered up to Rowan's face. "But maybe you could give me something to live for. I don't know. It's been years, and my life has been dedicated to hunting Kudlaks. In the beginning, I just wanted revenge, and the bloodier it was, the better, but that's changed. Over the years, I've come to realize that I'm doing a good thing. Kudlaks are dangerous. They kill and hurt people and don't care about the pain they leave behind. I don't want anyone to go through what I had to go through. If I can do anything to stop that from happening, then even if I die, it'll have been worth it."

This time, when he looked up, he didn't look down again. "But I know. I know how painful it is and how you wish you'd died with them some days. For a long time, the only thing that got me to get up in the evening was the thought that, eventually, I'd find the Kudlaks responsible for killing my family. And I will. I might not have found them yet, but eventually, I'll kill them with my own hands. Maybe then I'll decide I've had enough of hunting. I'm not too old yet, but I'm not as quick as I was when I was younger, and I've been wounded a few times. Being a hunter has taken its toll, and I'm not saying I want to do it for the rest of my life, but I can't stop until I find the Kudlaks who hurt my family."

Everything Clay was saying made sense, and Rowan had felt the same way for a long time. But he was past the need for revenge, while Clay wasn't. Rowan wasn't sure everything Clay had just said was enough for him to give his mate a chance.

Clay wasn't sure what he was trying to do. In part, he wanted to convince Rowan to hunt with him, but that wasn't all. Now that he'd found out he was Rowan's mate, he also wanted Rowan to give him a chance. He could see them together, hunting, then going home, watching each other's back, and spending the rest of their lives together. It might be foolish to rush that far ahead, but Clay had lost everything once in his life already. Now that he'd found Rowan, he wasn't about to make the mistake of letting him go.

But he wasn't sure Rowan would be willing to give him a

chance. Clay had tried to explain how he felt after everything that had happened to him and why he was doing all of this, and he suspected Rowan understood. They shared the same experience so maybe that would bring them together.

But it could as easily push them apart. Clay had reacted to losing his family by wanting revenge, but Rowan hadn't. He seemed almost afraid to do what he was born to do, and Clay remembered he'd yelled something about not wanting to lose someone else.

He understood. How could he not, after losing everyone? Since his family had been killed, Clay hadn't allowed himself to have anyone. In part, it was because it was easier now that he was a hunter, but there was also a part of him that, like Rowan, was afraid of what would happen if he came to care for someone else again.

Except Rowan wasn't human. He wasn't even just a shifter. He was a Krsnik, and Krsniks were born to hunt Kudlaks. If one person could survive this fight, it was him, and it gave Clay hope that they could make this work.

But for that to happen, Rowan would have to give him a chance, and Clay wasn't sure his mate would. That was why he was here. He'd been trying to give Rowan space because he was at work, but it seemed Rowan had had enough.

Clay supposed he was about to find out what would happen next between them.

His mouth was dry, so he took a sip of his beer. It was warm, but he didn't care. He also didn't care to look away from Rowan, who was staring back at him. He didn't seem surprised at what Clay had confessed just now. He'd probably heard this time and time again when he was a hunter, and Clay had met enough hunters to know that his story wasn't unheard of. Most hunters had become hunters because Kudlaks had hurt them or their families. They weren't born hunters like Krsniks. Something pushed them into becoming hunters, and usually, it was losing someone they loved.

"I understand what you went through," Rowan said slowly. "I went through it, too. I was where you are once. I wanted nothing more than revenge and to have Kudlak blood on my hands. I killed a lot of them after my family was decimated, but eventually, I realized it didn't matter. Even though I never caught the Kudlaks who hurt my family, even if I had, it wouldn't have changed anything. My family would still be dead. I'd still be alone in the world."

"You don't have to be alone." Clay hoped Rowan would decide not to be.

"Maybe you're right, and I don't have to, but what will happen if I say yes to you? We'll bond, then go on hunts. Eventually, one of us will get hurt. We'd be lucky if that's all that happens. What if one of us is killed? What if *you* are killed? I would lose the only person I have left, and I can't go through that again. I lost too much already. My heart wouldn't survive losing my mate, too."

Clay didn't want to choose between Rowan and hunting. He didn't want to give up either of them, but he didn't know if he could convince Rowan to go along with it.

He chose his words carefully because he didn't want Rowan to be angry. "And like you understand me, I understand you. I even behaved the way you did, isolating myself and keeping everyone away because I didn't want to care for new people in case they got killed. But eventually, I realized I couldn't live my life that way. Even if I promised never to hunt again, I could still die at any time. I could walk out of this bar, get struck by a car, or get mugged and shot. No one knows what the future holds, Rowan. No one can make any promises when it comes to death."

"There's a difference between being struck by a car and going out looking for trouble," Rowan pointed out.

"But we make a difference. Think about all the Kudlaks

I've killed. How many families could they have killed if I hadn't stopped them? How many children would have been orphaned, and how many hunters would that have created? I understand how frightened you are, and believe me, I'm scared every time I go out at night. At the same time, though, I know I'm doing a good thing. There was no one to save my family or yours, but you and I can save the families of people who won't have to become hunters and get revenge for the people they love. You can't ignore the world and how you can help it forever, Rowan, no matter how much you want to."

Rowan's shoulders were tense, but Clay felt good about the fact that he was listening. He didn't expect to change Rowan's mind tonight or tomorrow, but he needed Rowan to listen to him. They had different points of view, but it didn't mean either of them was right or wrong. In this situation, there *was* no right or wrong. Clay understood why Rowan had decided to step away from the hunter's life, and he was pretty sure Rowan understood why he hadn't, and they needed to find a way to match that together.

"Tell me about your family," Clay said when Rowan didn't answer.

Rowan looked around, but no one was paying attention to them. He sighed, then leaned back down. "It wasn't a single attack like in your case. You know what I am, so you understand that hunting is our entire life. From the time we're old enough to hold a knife, we're trained to go after Kudlaks. That's how my family died. One by one, they never returned from their hunt. Every time, the pain was the same, cutting into my heart. Those scars are still there, and while they've faded, they never disappeared. Every time I think about my family, it hurts."

"And not hunting helps with that?"

"Nothing helps with that."

It was incredible to Clay that an entire family of Krsniks

had vanished when they'd all been trained to kill Kudlaks. It even made him doubt that he was strong enough to continue hunting. He was only human, and while he'd survived until now, what were the odds that he'd survive for much longer, considering what had happened to Rowan's family? "They're all gone?"

"I think one of my cousins is still alive, or at least, that's what I heard." Rowan looked away. "But I haven't tried to find him."

"Why not?"

"Because what if the people who told me he was alive were wrong? What if he's dead, too?"

"You'd rather imagine him alive and happy somewhere than knowing he's dead."

"I guess."

Clay could understand that, yet at the same time, he couldn't. "You should try to find him. If he's the only member of your family still alive, I'm sure he'd be glad to hear from you. Maybe he thinks he's the only one left like you do."

"How would I find him? I wouldn't know where to start."

"Through the council. You guys are so rare that they have to know where he is." Clay wasn't sure this would help convince Rowan to give him a chance, but he wasn't doing this for him. Even if Rowan eventually rejected him, Clay wanted him to be happy.

That was why he'd suggested trying to find his cousin. He wanted Rowan to be happy, with or without him.

Rowan desperately wanted to find Emery. He'd wanted to find him since he'd heard about his cousin possibly being alive, but he was also terrified. What if he asked around and found out Emery was dead? If he didn't try to find him, he could live with the possibility that his cousin was somewhere out there, living his life. If he found out for sure that Emery was dead, he'd be losing the last member of his family, and like losing his mate, he didn't think his heart would survive that.

But it was tempting, especially with Clay pushing. Maybe that was all Clay was about. Rowan knew that some people believed shifters met their mates when they needed them the most. He wasn't quite sure why fate had decided he needed Clay now, especially considering Clay was a hunter. Even though he didn't want to, Rowan had to admit that maybe it was a sign that he needed to stop rejecting his heritage. That didn't mean he wanted to hunt again, but maybe it was time to make some changes.

Even though he barely knew Clay, he could tell the man was going to be incredibly smug when he agreed with him. He huffed because he might as well get it over with. "Fine. Maybe I do need to look for my cousin."

Clay beamed. "I can help you."

"Why would you?"

"Why do you think I'm here?"

"To convince me to hunt with you."

"Well, I won't deny that's part of it. I don't think I'd be your mate if you weren't meant to hunt again."

That was what Rowan had been thinking only seconds earlier. Fate didn't make mistakes, or at least that was what everyone said. Maybe she made a mistake when it came to Rowan, or maybe he was too stubborn to admit the truth.

He rubbed his face. He didn't know what to think or how to feel. He didn't want to admit he might have been wrong—and he definitely didn't want to become a hunter again.

But most of all, he didn't want to lose Clay.

Clay wasn't giving up, and Rowan doubted that anything he could say would push the human away. His best bet to get away from Clay—leave and never return. The only way Clay had to find him was to come to the bar, and if Rowan stopped working here, Clay wouldn't be able to get to him again.

The thought broke Rowan's heart a little. Even though he and Clay barely knew each other and had only met a few days ago, he already couldn't imagine a life without Clay. Finding another job, working at another bar without Clay sitting on the other side of the counter, was too hard to imagine. Rowan didn't want any of that to happen.

Where did that leave him? If he rejected Clay, he'd have to leave and never see his mate again. But if he decided to go along with all of this, he'd have to accept that Clay was a hunter. That might mean going on hunts to keep Clay safe. Was that something Rowan could do?

Physically, it wouldn't be a problem. He kept himself trained, and it had come in handy in certain situations, like the other night with the Kudlak. Going back to hunting meant being in danger again, though, and it meant possibly losing Clay.

So it was possibly losing Clay against definitely losing him. The choice shouldn't be as easy as it was considering the circumstances, but every fiber of Rowan's being wanted his mate. He was conflicted about going back to hunting, but he wanted to give Clay a chance.

"I'm not making promises," he said. Clay's eyes widened, and he started to smile, but Rowan raised a hand. "I left hunting for a reason, and I don't know if I can go back to it. I know I don't *want* to go back to it, but I also realize that might not be enough. Hunting doesn't have anything to do with the relationship between the two of us, though."

"So what you're saying is that you want us to see if we can be together, but you don't want to hunt."

"I don't know what I want at the moment. I just know that I can't push you away."

"Because I'm your mate."

"Yes. If you were anyone else, I wouldn't hesitate, but you're my mate." And to Rowan, who'd lost his family, it meant everything.

It meant not being alone anymore and having someone who loved him again. It also meant loving someone and putting his heart in jeopardy, but Rowan was starting to realize that would happen even if he left Clay behind. He'd always worry about his mate and wonder what Clay was up to.

Maybe it would be better if Rowan stuck close to protect him.

Clay had been gung-ho about them hunting together, but that wasn't what Rowan was offering. Maybe it wouldn't be enough for Clay. Maybe Clay would decide to leave Rowan behind after all.

But Clay was still smiling. "So you're giving us a chance?"

"I'm giving us as mates a chance. I'm not making promises when it comes to hunting. I understand what you're saying about keeping people safe, and I even agree with it. I just don't know if it's something I can do."

Clay snorted. "Please. We both know that you'll be right by my side the first time I try going on a hunt without you. You won't be able to stand me being away from you and possibly in danger when you can't do anything about it."

Rowan glared. How could this man—a man he'd just met—already know him that well? "I hate you."

Clay's smile grew. "I hate you, too, boo. I'm glad you're doing this, though."

Rowan sighed. "I'm pretty sure I'll regret it, but it's too late now."

"It was too late the day you met me and realized I was your mate."

Clay was right about that. There had been no escape for Rowan after meeting Clay, even though he'd tried to resist. He should probably have given in right away like Clay had suggested, but if he had, they wouldn't have had sex against the wall yesterday, and that had been hot as fuck. It wasn't something Rowan could regret, although he'd never admit that.

He had no idea what he was doing, but he could already tell life wouldn't be boring with Clay in it.

Clay caught Rowan's wrist like he had several times, but instead of using it to hold Rowan where he was, he twisted their hands until he could link their fingers together. Rowan glanced around, but no one was looking at them, not even Crystal. Even though he was at work, he and Clay were having a moment, and it sent his heart racing.

He'd been happy to find out about his mate, then terrified because of what Clay did. He was still afraid, but a part of him realized that agreeing to be with Clay would mean coming out of retirement. He'd never let Clay go on a hunt without him. If Clay was hunting Kudlaks, Rowan would be right there next to him, protecting him. He hadn't been able to do that for his family, but he could do it for Clay.

The fear of losing Clay was still there, but Rowan knew how to live with fear. He was always afraid when he faced Kudlaks, and that would never change. What he did with that fear could change, though. Until now, he'd allowed the fear to guide his steps. He'd allowed it to control him and his life, and it had been easy. It had even been comfortable, which wasn't something he associated with Clay. Clay was forcing him to face his fears, and while there was nothing he wanted less, maybe it wouldn't be a bad thing. Maybe it was what he'd needed from the beginning but hadn't known.

And maybe that was why fate had sent him Clay. It was time for Rowan to stop hiding, and the only person who could have pulled him out of it was his mate.

Clay was ridiculously happy. He was pretty sure that he was scaring some people in the bar with his idiotic smile, but how could he not feel this way?

He hadn't expected Rowan to give him anything tonight. If anything, he'd expected Rowan to push back, tell him to leave, and refuse to even talk to him. It was clear that Clay's presence in Rowan's life reminded Rowan of everything he'd lost, and Clay was sorry about that, but he truly believed they could work together and that they wouldn't be mates if that wasn't true. He only needed Rowan to give him a chance, and apparently, Rowan had decided to do just that.

"What now?" Clay asked, squeezing Rowan's hand.

Rowan stared at their linked fingers for a moment. "Well, you could let me go, considering I'm at work."

"Right. Can you give me another beer?"

Rowan appeared exasperated, which was an expression Clay often saw on the faces of the people who had to deal with him. He could be a little too much sometimes, but considering he was Rowan's mate, it meant Rowan was perfectly capable of handling it.

Rowan turned to get Clay another beer, and Clay watched him. He didn't know what would come next for them, but he did know that if Rowan was going to protect him, he'd have to come out on hunts with him. Clay usually worked on his own, mostly because he'd realized it was better to only rely on himself, but he trusted Rowan, and not just because he was a Krsnik. Maybe it was the bond between them, or maybe the experience Rowan had when it came to hunting Kudlaks. Whatever the case, Clay was glad to have found a partner.

And he had no doubt that was what they would be. They weren't just mates. They'd hunt together, rid the world of Kudlaks, and hopefully find the ones who'd killed their families. Clay wasn't looking for revenge anymore, but he couldn't let this go. Knowing they were out there, hurting other families and destroying people's lives, was enough of an incentive for him to want to kill them. Avenging his family would be a bonus, but it wasn't the main reason he was in this.

Rowan placed the beer in front of Clay, who took it with a smile.

"So tell me about yourself."

Rowan arched a brow. "Is that how you usually attempt to seduce guys?"

Clay laughed. "I don't have to seduce anyone. I wiggle my fingers, and they fall at my feet."

"Do they?"

Rowan sounded amused, so Clay decided they needed to get to know each other without the heavy weight of hunting on their shoulders. They'd always be hunters, but maybe they could just be Clay and Rowan tonight. "I swear they do." Clay raised his fingers and wiggled them at Rowan. "Is it working?"

Rowan was trying to hide his smile, but Clay had seen it and wanted more. He wanted Rowan to forget about the Kudlaks for the night, and he didn't care if he made himself look silly to do so. Rowan was conflicted over becoming a hunter again, and maybe, he needed to see that wasn't all their relationship would be about.

When it came to it, if Clay had to choose between Rowan and hunting right now, he'd choose hunting, but he was pretty sure that wouldn't be true in a very short while. He liked Rowan, and once they started spending time together, it wouldn't be hard for him to fall in love with his mate. By the time he was, he'd choose Rowan over pretty much anything, including hunting, but he didn't think Rowan realized that. If he did, he wouldn't have hesitated so much about giving in to Clay.

But Clay wasn't planning to stop his pursuit of Rowan

anytime soon. He'd hunt Kudlaks for as long as he could, and then, who knew? He and Rowan would find out together. "Well, I don't have to be charming anymore, do I? I've already gotten you."

"Oh?"

"I'm your mate. I don't have to seduce you."

"You better at least try if you don't want to sleep on the couch."

Clay's heart stuttered. "Oh? Is that your way of asking me if I want to come back to yours tonight?"

"I'm pretty sure you were always going to come home with me tonight." He hesitated. "To sleep. I can't let you leave after what happened, but I need a little time."

He was probably right. Clay hadn't expected things to go this smoothly when he'd decided to come back to the bar a third time and try talking to Rowan, but he liked their banter. He liked that Rowan was relaxing, and he knew he'd been right to think that Rowan needed this. Maybe he did, too.

Clay had been a hunter for a long time now, and he hadn't allowed himself to care for people. It had felt dangerous, although he'd changed his mind about that a while ago. He couldn't just be a hunter. That way lay madness and the inability to see right from wrong. He'd seen it happen with hunters blinded by revenge so severely that it was the only thing they cared about. They hated Kudlaks, and they killed them indiscriminately. They didn't believe Kudlaks could be anything but monsters, and in general, Clay agreed.

But he'd seen many things over the years since he'd become a hunter. He'd seen humans behaving as much like monsters as Kudlaks, and that was one more reason he was still hunting. If he could keep an eye on the other hunters, maybe, he could keep more than humans safe. The Kudlaks weren't the only supernatural creatures out there, and some hunters didn't see a difference between them and normal shifters.

A customer reached the counter, and Rowan turned to talk to him. Clay didn't try to stop him. He realized Rowan was working and that this job was important to him at the moment. Eventually, he'd have to quit, but for now, Clay was more than happy to relax on his stool and watch his mate move around.

There was a grace in every one of Rowan's movements, almost as if he was dancing. Watching him fight felt the same way, and Clay wondered if he moved that way because of the training he'd gone through. He'd mentioned he'd been training since he was old enough to hold a knife, which would make sense, since Krsniks were born to hunt Kudlaks. Clay had many more questions about them, and it looked like he'd have the opportunity to ask eventually.

But not tonight. Tonight was about Clay and Rowan, about the men they were and the future they would share. Hunting would be a big part of it, but not the only part, and Clay had every intention of showing Rowan that.

Reality would be there tomorrow night, too. There were plenty of Kudlaks out there, hurting and killing people. They wouldn't stop just because Clay and Rowan had met, and while it made Clay slightly anxious to feel like he was wasting an evening, he couldn't regret it. He and Rowan both needed this. Clay would be back at it tomorrow, stronger than ever and ready to take on the world.

And with Rowan by his side.

CHAPTER FOUR

*W*e *can confirm that Emery Harper is currently living with the Whitedell Pride. We can't provide you with a phone number, but if you'd like to contact him, please let us know. We'll reach out to him and ensure he gets the message.*

Rowan stared at the email. He hadn't expected much when he'd seen that the council had emailed him back, but he'd been wrong.

So wrong.

He swallowed, unable to look away from his phone. He hadn't had much hope when he'd emailed the council's department of family reunion that had been created after what had happened with the labs and everything. It had felt like the easiest way to find out more about Emery, but Rowan hadn't expected this.

His cousin was alive. He was currently living in Whitedell.

What was Rowan supposed to do with this information?

His first instinct was to call Clay. That didn't surprise him, even though he and Clay didn't know each other well. They were mates, and Clay had been the one who gently pushed Rowan in the direction of contacting the council. He'd want to know about the email, and Rowan had every intention of telling him.

But he already knew what Clay would suggest. He'd want Rowan to pack up his things and go straight to Whitedell, and Rowan wasn't sure he was ready for that. Part of him yearned to find Emery, but another part was terrified of what he'd find. Emery was alive, yes, but would he want to see Rowan?

Rowan hadn't looked for Emery in all these years, too afraid of what he'd find. Why hadn't Emery looked for Rowan?

Maybe he had. It wasn't like Rowan had kept up with the council, and living on his own, it had been easy for him not to let them know where he was—or even that he existed. It seemed Emery was living with the pride, though, and those were registered with the council, this one especially, considering the alpha was a council member. Clay was going to have kittens when he learned about this. Rowan already had so many questions, and he hadn't even seen his cousin yet.

Why was Emery living with the pride? He didn't have a family, just like Rowan, and maybe he'd needed the company. He'd gone the opposite way from Rowan, who'd isolated himself. Rowan doubted Emery was still hunting Kudlaks, but if he was, at least he had support.

But what if Emery was happy with the life he had? Would he want to see Rowan? Or would Rowan just be a reminder of everything Emery had lost? Emery would certainly remind Rowan of all the people who'd died, but that didn't mean he didn't want to see his cousin. He couldn't be sure the same would go for Emery, and the last thing he wanted was to hurt his cousin. If he'd built himself a life in Whitedell, Rowan didn't want to bother him or remind him of things better forgotten.

He groaned and thumped the back of his head against the couch. There was mold in the corner of the ceiling, and he stared at the spot for a moment, trying to put his thoughts into order. Okay, so he knew where his cousin was. He knew Emery was safe, alive, and probably okay. If he was part of the Whitedell pride, it meant he was protected. He didn't need Rowan, but that didn't mean he wouldn't want to see him. If he was like Rowan, he'd been worried about Rowan for a long time now, and while he hadn't reached out, it might be because, like Rowan, he'd been afraid, or maybe because he hadn't known Rowan was alive.

Where did this leave Rowan?

His phone vibrated in his hand, and he peered at the screen, foolishly wondering if it could be Emery. Rowan hadn't left his phone number in the email, so it would be impossible for Emery to call. Sure enough, it was Clay's name on the screen.

Rowan didn't hesitate to answer. Clay had been worming his way into Rowan's life, and while Rowan hadn't been sure it was the best idea in the beginning—and still wasn't—he couldn't imagine his life without Clay anymore. Clay clearly knew what he was doing and was making sure Rowan couldn't live without him.

He'd succeeded, mostly.

"Hi," Rowan said when he answered.

There was a pause before Clay answered back. "What happened?"

"Nothing."

"That's bullshit. I can hear it in your voice."

Rowan went back to staring at the ceiling. How could Clay have noticed? They hadn't known each other long enough that he should be able to read Rowan's tone, especially on the phone. Yet, here they were, with Clay knowing something was up. It was no use telling him no, because he'd push and prod until Rowan was honest and admitted the truth. When he wanted something, he didn't let go until he got it.

Rowan sighed. "I emailed the council a few days ago."

"Okay, and? What did you email them about?"

"My cousin. I wanted to find out if they knew where he was."

Clay sucked in a breath. "Do they?"

"Yeah. Of course, they can't let me contact him directly, but they know where he is. He's in Whitedell, with the pride there."

"What are we waiting for, then?"

Rowan found himself smiling. He'd known Clay would react this way. "He might not want to see me."

"Why wouldn't he want to? I'm sure he's been wondering what happened to you the entire time you've been wondering what happened to him."

"Possibly, but he has a life there. I don't know how long he's been in Whitedell, but I haven't seen him in twenty years."

"You're that old, huh?"

Rowan rolled his eyes. "You know how it goes with shifters."

"Yeah, yeah. You're robbing the cradle here, sweetheart."

"I am not. You're not a child."

"Not a child, but twenty-five years old is quite young, isn't it?"

It was, and it was young to have gone through what Clay had gone through, but there was nothing Rowan could do about that. He could only try to make Clay happy now that they were together.

The problem was that he wasn't quite sure they were together. They'd had sex against the wall in the parking lot and agreed to see where things could go between them, but so far, they hadn't gone on a date or anything like that. They didn't need to date to be together, but they'd only seen each other at the bar, and while they'd had some deep conversations, it didn't mean they fit well together as a couple. Clay seemed intent on finding out, though, and while Rowan was more hesitant, he was hopeful.

"Look," Clay said. "You've done the hard thing. You've contacted the council and found out your cousin is alive. Now you only have to jump in your car, drive there, and see him. I don't see why he wouldn't want to see you, but even if he doesn't, you'll know he's all right. Isn't that what you always wanted?"

"Of course."

"Then allow him to decide whether or not he wants to see you. He should be the one to decide, not you."

"And you feel that by deciding not to go, I'm keeping that choice from him." Clay wasn't wrong. Emery should be the one to decide if he wanted to see Rowan, and since he didn't know Rowan was alive, he wouldn't be able to do that until Rowan reached out. It was scary, but it also felt right to take that first step.

"I'll call the bar as soon as I'm done with this phone call," Rowan said. He couldn't help but smile. "I'm sure Tommy will be fine with me taking a few days, or maybe even more."

"I think you should quit your job and move to Whitedell."

Rowan wasn't surprised. Clay was impulsive and followed his emotions rather than allowing them to hold him back. It was something Rowan envied him for. He'd always been cautious, but especially so after he'd lost his family. "Let me talk to Emery first and see what he says. I don't want to move there if he doesn't want me around."

"He'll want you," Clay promised. "And I'm coming with you."

Rowan had expected that, too. "Don't you have anything to do here?"

"Not really. I was working in a grocery store, but I can quit easily, and I'm sure there are Kudlaks in Whitedell or close to it. I'll be fine."

He probably would be. Clay struck Rowan as someone who was usually fine, whatever happened. It was impressive, and something Rowan wished he could do.

"All right. You can come with me."

"Road trip!" Clay yelled.

Rowan rolled his eyes. This was going to be an experience, wasn't it?

Half an hour later, Clay was ready. It hadn't taken much. He was used to moving every few years, sometimes even more frequently, so he didn't own a lot. Everything fit into two bags. Quitting his job at the grocery store had been easy. There were a few people in town he'd wanted to say goodbye to, but a phone call had been just fine. He'd found out that his neighbor's car had broken down, so he'd decided to leave his to the woman. She cried when he told her, but he didn't need a car. Rowan would be the one driving most of the way, and while Clay's car was a piece of junk, Rowan's was nice. If Clay needed a car, he could get a new one once they were in Whitedell.

He had no doubt they'd both end up moving there. Rowan was hesitant, which was understandable, but Clay wasn't. The only family Rowan had left was in Whitedell, and there was no one out there anywhere for Clay. It made sense that both of them would move there so Rowan could be close to Emery. There probably wouldn't be any Kudlaks in the town itself since Emery lived there, but there were towns around Whitedell that Clay could explore. Like always, he'd find a way. At least this time, he wouldn't be alone, because Rowan would be with him.

It was strange, but it also felt good. Clay had been living alone for a long time. His family had been attacked when he was seventeen, but he'd been lucky enough to turn eighteen while he was in the hospital. He'd never ended up in foster care. As soon as he was well enough to leave the hospital, he'd been on his own, and that hadn't changed, even after seven years. It felt like a long time for him, so finding out that Rowan had lived alone for at least twenty years had shocked him. He understood why but wasn't sure he could have done it. Besides, in twenty years, he'd probably be in too bad of a shape to hunt Kudlaks. He wouldn't be old by any means, but he already had a few old wounds and scars that bothered him when he pushed himself too hard. They weren't going to get better, and he was glad he wouldn't be hunting alone anymore and that when he decided to retire, it wouldn't be to an empty house. Rowan gave him a reason to stop hunting Kudlaks, and while he wasn't ready to do so yet, he wouldn't hunt until he died.

He and Rowan had agreed to meet at the bar, so Clay had asked his neighbor to give him a ride there. She'd been more than happy to do so, and Clay had watched his car disappear around the corner. He wasn't leaving anyone or anything behind, and that was fine with him.

He stared at the sky as he waited for Rowan. He'd seen Rowan's car in the parking lot, which meant Rowan was inside, telling his boss he was quitting. Or maybe he was just taking some time off. Clay had suggested he quit outright, but Rowan was understandably more cautious.

Clay beamed when the back door opened and Rowan appeared. Rowan scowled at him, but there was no heat in it, and it didn't last long.

"Hey, honeybun," Clay said as he moved toward Rowan.

The scowl reappeared. "Don't call me that."

"Why not?" Clay asked before smacking a kiss on Rowan's cheek. Rowan blinked as if he wasn't quite sure what to make of this. He probably wasn't, but it was fun to tease him.

"Because it's a ridiculous name for a grown man," Rowan said as he pushed Clay toward his car.

Clay opened the passenger door and threw his bags in the backseat before sliding in. "I don't see why not. Honeybun is a perfectly fine name."

"I'm not your honey bun."

Clay sighed heavily, but he wasn't done teasing. "Fine. How about sugarplum?"

If looks could have killed, he'd already be dead.

"Neither of them." Rowan was trying to keep his voice harsh, but he couldn't seem to help the smile on his lips. He was having fun, which meant Clay would continue.

It felt good to be like this with someone. Even though there had been a good reason for Clay to be alone, he'd missed the company. He'd missed having someone to talk to, tease, and smile with. He wasn't an idiot, and he knew that Rowan wasn't sure about where things would go between them, but he was giving him a chance, and that was all Clay needed. He'd convince Rowan they should be together and that they should move to Whitedell, and then, a new chapter of their lives could begin.

"What did your boss say?" he asked.

"He wasn't happy to see me go, but he understood when I explained."

"Did you quit or take time off?"

Rowan hesitated. "I quit. I promised that if things didn't go well, I'd be back, and he seemed relieved, but he knows that if my cousin is happy to see me, I'll be staying there."

"That's good."

"Do we have to return to your apartment to grab more things? Not that you have to move to Whitedell with me." Rowan hurried to add.

"Oh, I'm moving. And don't worry about my things. Everything is in the backseat."

Rowan quickly looked back, arching a brow at the sight of Clay's two bags. There already had been a few bags in the backseat, and the trunk was probably full. Still, neither of them had much, which made it easy to move at the drop of a hat like they were doing.

It took them about half a day to reach Whitedell, and Rowan was silent most of the time. Clay didn't push him to talk. He could only imagine what was going through Rowan's head, and he could feel his mate needed the time and space. Clay wasn't usually one to be silent, but he played on his phone, looked out the window, and just wasted time and allowed Rowan to be with his thoughts. Once they crossed into Whitedell, though, all bets were off.

"Do you know where the pride lives?" he asked, looking around.

The town was cute, and even though it wasn't that small, it had a small-town feeling. They were driving down Main Street, and the stores lining both sides were adorable and full of people. The surprising thing was the demons walking down the sidewalk. Clay had never seen one in real life before, but he knew about them. They were part of the supernatural community but usually kept to themselves.

But not in Whitedell.

"I looked into it before leaving," Rowan said.

He continued to drive and appeared to know where he was going, so Clay relaxed.

He managed until they turned onto a small road and found themselves in front of the gate. They'd arrived, and there was no way for either of them to know what was about to happen.

Rowan froze in his seat, but Clay didn't have a problem taking the next step. He climbed out of the car, ignored his mate calling for him, and rang the bell. He only had to wait a moment for someone to answer. "Yes?" a man asked.

"Hi. My name is Clay, and I'm here with my mate, Rowan. We're looking for Emery Harper."

"What do you want with Emery?"

"Rowan is his cousin."

"One moment."

Clay nodded, then turned back to the car. Rowan was glaring at him, but Clay didn't care. He beamed, knowing he'd done the right thing, and gave his mate a little wave.

That was why they were together, wasn't it? When one of

them was unable to do something, the other would be there to help or do it for them.

There was a click, and the gate started to open. Clay climbed back into the car, and while Rowan was clearly nervous, he smiled. Once the gate was open, he slowly drove through it, then toward the massive house they could see in the distance.

Clay had known the place would be big because it housed an entire pride, but he hadn't expected this. It was impressive, and while it wasn't somewhere he'd enjoy living because of the many people there, it was absolutely beautiful.

The front door opened before they could get out of the car. A tall man stood there, staring at them with his arms crossed over his chest. He waited until they were out of the car to come down the stone steps, then offered Rowan his hand since he was closest to him. "I'm Nate, the pride's beta."

Rowan shook his hand. "I'm Rowan."

"Emery's cousin."

"That would be me, yes," Rowan confirmed. "And this is my mate, Clay."

It thrilled Clay to have Rowan claim him like that. He hadn't expected it, but he loved it.

"You look like your cousin," Nate said.

Clay went to stand next to Rowan, who leaned against him. Clay wasn't sure Rowan knew he was doing it, but that was okay.

"He's here, then?" Rowan asked.

"He is, and he agreed to see you. Follow me."

They did.

The house was massive and gorgeous, but Rowan could barely see it as he and Clay followed Nate through it. He could hear people walking and talking around the house, and he was curious, but all of his thoughts were focused on Emery.

He was here. He wanted to see Rowan. It was more than Rowan had expected, and his legs felt like jelly as he walked. He'd hoped for this for a long time and could hardly believe he finally had it.

Nate eventually paused in front of a door. Rowan wasn't sure he'd be able to find the front door again if he had to because the house was so big and intricate. Nate hadn't had a problem finding the door, but this was his home.

"Emery is in here," Nate explained. "The room is quiet, and you can stay here for as long as you want, but I won't be far."

That was a warning that if Rowan tried hurting Emery, Nate wouldn't hesitate to step in. It made sense since he was the beta and Emery was part of his pride.

"I'm not here to hurt him," Rowan promised.

Nate nodded, then quickly knocked and opened the door. Rowan sucked in a breath. He didn't know how Emery would react to seeing him, but he was about to find out. Once he did, he could move forward.

He stepped into the room. He only had a moment to look around before something slammed against him. He raised his hands to catch that something, and his eyes burned when he realized it was his cousin. Emery wrapped himself around Rowan, and Rowan held Emery close, the tears finally coming down.

It had been more than twenty years — twenty years of loneliness, of believing he was alone, of wondering if the rest of his life would be empty of people. Finding Clay had felt like a miracle, but this was almost better.

"Oh my god," Emery said. "When Nate told me, I didn't believe him. I thought you were dead. I thought everyone was dead."

Emery sobbed, and Rowan clung to him. He knew how his

cousin was feeling. He'd thought everyone was dead, too, and knowing he was alone in the world had been so painful. "I'm the only one left," he croaked, not wanting Emery to think there was anyone else left. He knew how much it hurt to hope for nothing.

Emery leaned back. "We are, you mean."

"Yeah."

Emery still looked the same. They'd always been told they looked like each other, and they did. They had the same dark hair and violet eyes, and while Rowan was taller, they could have passed for twins. Twenty years had passed, but that hadn't changed.

"And we're not alone," Emery added, taking Rowan's hand to pull him into the room. "Come meet my mate and our children."

Rowan blinked. Emery had kids?

A man had been sitting on one of the couches, but he got up when Emery and Rowan reached him. He was taller than Rowan's six foot one height, and his red hair gleamed in the soft yellow light that illuminated the room. His skin was pale and freckled, and his smile was kind and welcoming.

And he had a little boy in his arms.

The boy was sleeping. He couldn't be more than two or three years old, although Rowan had never been great with guessing how old kids were. He also couldn't guess how old the girl sitting on the floor by the coffee table was.

"This is Troy, my mate," Emery explained. "And our son, Matthew. And this is Hazel, our girl. Our oldest lives in Gillham with his mate, but I hope that you'll meet him soon. Aaron will be happy to know he has a cousin."

Clay cleared his throat. "Two cousins. Hi, I'm Clay, Rowan's mate."

Rowan was so overwhelmed that he'd forgotten to introduce Clay. What kind of mate did that make him? But Clay didn't seem to care, and after introducing himself to Emery and Troy, he wrapped an arm around Rowan's waist and held him close. It flustered Rowan because he wasn't used to being in this kind of proximity with anyone, but it felt nice, and he needed the support.

"I never expected anything like this to happen," Emery said as he sat down.

Troy sat next to him, their son still in his arms. They were a beautiful family, and Rowan thought the boy looked like both his fathers, even though it was impossible. He was certainly Troy's biological son, though, with his red hair.

"I thought I'd lost everyone," Rowan told him. "I'd heard that you were alive, but I was afraid to ask the council if they knew anything."

Emery nodded. "You thought I might be dead anyway, and you didn't want to know for sure. I had no idea you were alive. I—when I lost my father, well, he was the last family member in our family unit, and I couldn't stay around. The clan would have kept me, but I couldn't. It was easier to stay behind. I just wish I'd looked for you. It was so hard back then, though, and everything was a mess even after I moved here."

Troy took one of Emery's hands, which didn't look comfortable with their son still in his arms. "That was entirely my fault. Emery had to focus on me for a while, and then we had Aaron. It was a lot."

Rowan leaned forward. "I don't blame you, Em. I'm glad to see you so happy and with a family." Most Krsniks didn't live long enough to meet their mate or have kids. Emery had, and even though it had kept him away from Rowan, Rowan didn't resent him for any of it.

"What about you? Do you have kids?" Emery asked.

"No. It was just me until a week ago, actually. Then Clay barged into my life, almost got himself killed by a Kudlak, and convinced me to find you."

And here they were. Rowan finally allowed himself to relax. Emery was okay. He was happy, and he was glad to see Rowan. This had gone the best way it could have, and Rowan didn't have to be afraid anymore.

He didn't know how long they talked. Troy and Clay were mostly silent, which in Clay's case was a minor miracle. Matthew eventually woke up and went to play with his sister, who sprouted wings for a surprising handful of seconds. Rowan had so many questions that he couldn't keep them straight, but they didn't matter.

"You don't live in Whitedell," Emery eventually said.

"Not yet, but we're moving," Clay answered, ignoring Rowan's glare.

Emery grinned. "I see. Well, whether or not you're moving here, I'm not going anywhere, Ro. Whenever you want to talk to or see me, you know where to find me. I'm not letting you go now that I found you. We might both have lost the family we had growing up, but we have a new one now."

Rowan realized Emery meant that his family was also Rowan's, and it brought tears to his eyes again. How had he gone from being completely alone to having a mate, his cousin, and a bunch of other people in his life? And in just a few days, too. It was all thanks to Clay, and while Rowan had been hesitant before, now, he wanted nothing more than to bond with Clay.

He was never letting Clay go, even though it meant he'd have to start hunting again. Clay was his — to love and protect.

Clay was glad the Whitedell alpha had offered him and Rowan a room for the night. He'd tried offering two rooms, but Rowan had refused without even looking at Clay. Clay hadn't argued. He wanted to spend the night with Rowan, and he was giddy at the thought of what could happen between them. Their one time against the wall at the bar hadn't been nearly enough for him, but he had high hopes.

He wasn't used to being surrounded by people, let alone an entire pride. It was incredibly noisy and busy, especially when it was time for dinner, and Clay kept himself aside. Rowan couldn't do the same because Emery was dragging him around the dining room to introduce him to anyone who appeared willing to say hello. Rowan was clearly overwhelmed, and Clay was pretty sure he'd run if he could, but instead, he went along with Emery, nodding and smiling. He'd probably do anything Emery asked of him, which was adorable and made Clay miss his family even more.

"You're new," a pink-haired man said as he flopped into the chair next to Clay.

Clay didn't know who the guy was, but the expression on his face didn't bode well. He looked to the other side just in time to find another man sliding into the chair there.

He was surrounded.

Clay glanced at Rowan, but he was busy with Emery, which meant Clay was on his own. For some reason, these two men scared him more than a pack of Kudlaks. Clay didn't like their vibes, even though he doubted they were dangerous. They were pride members, after all.

"He's with Emery's cousin," the second guy said.

Clay cleared his throat. "I'm Clay, Rowan's mate. Uh, Rowan's Emery's cousin."

Pink-hair grinned. "So you're family."

"I wouldn't quite say that."

"But I would. I'm Nysys, your new cousin, and this is Keenan."

"Cousin?"

"Well, we're not related or anything like that, but yeah. I feel like I'm your cousin. Maybe twice removed? I never understood how that worked."

"We're not the same species," Clay pointed out. Nysys was a Nix, even though he had pink hair. His pointed ears were a clear sign.

"Who cares? I certainly don't. Besides, your mate isn't human, yet the two of you are together."

"Because we're mates."

"And we're cousins."

Clay gave up. It was obvious there would be no reasoning with Nysys, and he was pretty sure he'd get a headache if he tried. "Sure. Let's go with that." Clay could tell he and Rowan would spend a lot of time in Whitedell, which meant spending time with Nysys. It could only be good to have allies, and besides, Clay wasn't opposed to getting a new family.

It was nice not to be alone in the world anymore.

Dinner was a lot, and Clay was happy when it was over. He wasn't as happy when Nysys volunteered to show him and Rowan their room, but he went along with it because he doubted he had a choice.

Nysys chatted all the way up the stairs and along the hallways. Clay wasn't paying attention until Nysys said, "And then, it exploded."

"What exploded?" Clay asked.

Nysys arched a blond brow. "Weren't you listening?"

"I, uh, I got lost. Sorry."

Thankfully, Nysys didn't appear offended. "That's fine. Most people don't listen to me when I talk. Anyway, the cake exploded. Don't ask me how I did it because I have no idea, but I was banned from the kitchen for an entire month after that. Can you believe it?"

Clay could, and he was glad he hadn't accepted a piece of that cake in the kitchen when Troy had offered it to him. He made a mental note never to accept any food Nysys offered.

"There you go," Nysys said, stopping in front of a door. "If you don't like this room, I can find you another one. We have plenty."

"This will be fine," Rowan said. He pushed open the door and disappeared into the room without a backward glance.

Clay looked back at Nysys. "Sorry about that. He had an eventful day."

Nysys didn't seem offended. "I get it. We all do. The Whitedell pride is a mix of people who didn't have a home before and found one here. We all understand what you and Rowan have been through, even without having details."

Clay wasn't sure about that, but he nodded anyway. He was relieved when Nysys left, but he didn't know what was waiting for him inside the room.

The answer was nothing. Rowan was nowhere to be seen, which explained the sound of the shower running in the bathroom. Clay had no idea what Rowan would want or how he'd feel when he was done, so he decided to focus on himself. He stripped, dumped his jeans and t-shirt on a chair, and slipped into bed. He could skip brushing his teeth for one night.

Rowan took much longer than Clay had expected, but it was worth seeing him leave the bathroom wearing only a towel. Clay couldn't look away, and he didn't try to hide it. It was useless because he suspected Rowan had asked for only one room for a reason.

And Clay was about to find out what that reason was.

Rowan stopped at the foot of the bed and stared. Clay stared back, knowing it would be easier to give Rowan the space he needed to get out whatever he was about to say. Things could be difficult between them, but Clay didn't want that to happen. Since the problems usually started when he opened his mouth, he didn't.

"I want us to bond," Rowan eventually said.

That wasn't what Clay had expected. He continued staring as he tried to make sense of the words, but he already knew what they meant. "I . . ." he croaked, unable to say anything else.

"I realize it's probably too soon, but it's the one condition I have to hunt with you. If we're bonded, we'll be able to tell that the other is in danger and act accordingly. I'm sorry if you wanted it to be more romantic, but I can't go back out without a full bond."

Clay needed to answer before Rowan thought he was saying no. "All right."

"I don't know how things will work between us, but we'll figure it out."

"I said yes, Rowan." Clay sat up and held out a hand. "Come here."

Clay had never thought about bonding, but he knew how it worked. He'd even watched some fake bonding porn after meeting Rowan, and while he knew things would be different because their bond was real, he had the basics down. Sex, then biting and blood-drinking, and they'd be bonded.

Easy, right?

Rowan snapped his mouth shut. He stared for a moment, then took a step forward. The towel slipped from his waist, and when he reached Clay, he was naked, which was perfect.

Rowan was perfect.

Clay had no doubt they'd fight, maybe hate each other sometimes, but they could do this. He had faith in both of them.

"Come here," Clay repeated.

Rowan obeyed. He climbed onto the bed, making no secret what he was after. Clay was already sliding off his underwear as Rowan slid the sheet off him, and when he settled in front of Clay, Clay opened his legs to give him access. He didn't know how Rowan liked sex, but he was about to find out.

Rowan sucked him down without hesitation. Clay let him do whatever he wanted. He was at his mercy, and he'd take whatever Rowan wanted to do. He tangled his hand into Rowan's soft hair, barely able to see its color in the darkness of the room, but he didn't need to. He already knew Rowan was beautiful.

Rowan slid his hands under Clay's ass and pulled him closer. He never stopped sucking and lavishing Clay's cock with attention, and Clay wondered if this would be enough for them to bond. Sex wasn't needed, but that was when it usually happened. And where would Rowan bite him? On the neck like was usual, or maybe on the thigh? That was what had happened in that porn, and it had made Clay hot all over, but he also wouldn't mind having a mate mark that people could see.

Rowan squeezed Clay's ass harder, bringing Clay's attention back to him. Clay grinned and pulled at Rowan's hair as he fucked Rowan's mouth in short, quick bursts. Watching Rowan was a spectacle Clay knew he'd never get enough of. His cock was slick between Rowan's lips, and he could already feel the tingle of pleasure in his groin.

He should have known it wouldn't be that easy.

Rowan let go of Clay's cock with a pop, then moved up and leaned over him. He kissed his stomach, then looked up. His gaze told Clay he thought Clay was the greatest thing that had ever happened to him, and Clay felt the same way when it came to him. He didn't know how to say the words and make Rowan see that, but he wasn't sure he should — or could. He hadn't expected to feel so strongly about anyone, not even his mate, and he was startled to realize he couldn't imagine life without Rowan anymore. He'd say yes to anything as long as they could be together, even if Rowan asked Clay to stop hunting.

Rowan lifted Clay's leg and kissed his ankle. Clay stared. He had no idea what Rowan was doing. He'd expected this to be quick since Rowan had bonding in mind, but that wasn't what Rowan was doing.

"What are you doing?" Clay asked.

"I'm taking care of you."

Rowan's lips drifted over Clay's skin, up his leg, then his stomach. His touch was light, but it was the only thing Clay could feel.

No one had ever taken care of Clay like this. When he'd still had his family, he'd been too young to be in a relationship, and afterward, he'd kept everyone away. He'd only had quick fucks in bathrooms and dark alleys, and he'd been fine with that. He hadn't needed anyone, and he still didn't.

Except that wasn't true. Now that he'd met Rowan, he knew that everyone needed someone, even him. It felt good to have Rowan focus on him. He felt a bit self-conscious and didn't know what to do, but Rowan didn't seem to care.

Clay had never realized that making love could feel like this. He let Rowan do what he wanted, eager to feel more and to find out what else Rowan was planning for him. He could tell Rowan needed some control, and he was enjoying this too much to push his mate away. He usually preferred being in control, but when it came to Rowan, this was perfect, too.

Rowan moved up Clay's body. He kissed Clay's lips, then his jaw. Clay had been about to come before, but the pleasure had slightly faded after Rowan had stopped sucking him. It was coming back with a vengeance, and Clay needed more.

"What do you want?" Rowan asked.

"Whatever you want."

Rowan chuckled and lightly bit down on one of Clay's nipples. "So I can fuck you?"

Clay didn't usually fuck. There was never enough time, and he didn't want to do that in a club bathroom. For Rowan, though, he was ready to say yes. He knew Rowan would take care of him like he had until now.

"Stop worrying," Rowan whispered. "We can do it the

other way around if you want. Anything's good with me as long as I do it with you."

"No, I want to do it. I mean, yes, you can fuck me. Please." Clay felt like an idiot, but it made Rowan smile, so it was worth it.

"I'll take care of you," Rowan promised.

"I know."

Clay's mouth went dry when Rowan pushed his legs apart. Like he'd promised, he took good care of Clay. Clay slightly tensed when Rowan pressed a finger against his hole. It was slick, and the sensation made Clay arch a brow.

"Where did you get the lube?"

"Your new cousin, Nysys. He slipped it in my hand while you were talking to Troy just before we left the dining room."

Maybe it wouldn't be that bad to have cousins.

"He's not my cousin," Clay said to distract himself from the strange sensation in his lower body.

"That's what he introduced himself to me as. I'm sure he said he was your new cousin."

"I guess the pride has already adopted us."

The sensation of having something inside him had been odd in the beginning, but now that Clay was relaxing, it actually felt nice.

Clay felt the moment when Rowan added a third finger because it stung, but it was nothing he couldn't stand. His cock was still hard as fuck, and he wanted more.

Rowan gave him that when he twisted his fingers and brushed against Clay's prostate.

Clay cried out and grabbed Rowan's forearm. Rowan stopped moving, but that wasn't what Clay wanted, so he let go. Rowan grinned at him, then went back to driving Clay nuts. Clay wasn't sure he'd survive if this was what their mating would be like.

But Rowan didn't start moving again. Instead, he reached

for his own cock, and Clay knew it was time.

Finally.

Rowan stretched out between Clay's legs. He kissed him, probably to distract him. It worked because there was almost no pain when he finally slid into Clay. It was tight and hot, at the brink of being too much, but it was perfectly enough.

It felt *good*.

Then Rowan kissed Clay, and it became even better. Clay gave himself over, trusting his mate to take care of him. It was an odd feeling, but if there was one person Clay could give up control to, it was Rowan. So when Rowan leaned down toward Clay's neck, Clay surrendered completely. He tilted his head, not surprised when Rowan didn't hesitate. He'd been the one to ask for this, after all.

Fangs sank into Clay's flesh, making him jerk back. It was hard to worry about the pain when Rowan gave Clay so much pleasure.

Clay's back arched on one particular thrust of Rowan's. The drag and slight burn were satisfying and felt so good that Clay thought he was about to come. They weren't done yet, though. Rowan was drinking Clay's blood, but Clay hadn't had Rowan's, and even though he was human, he wanted it.

Rowan seemed to read Clay's mind because he raised a hand, and with a flash of movement, blood beaded on his neck. Clay hesitated, but only for a moment. He wanted this, maybe as much as Rowan did. Their lives would change after this, and it was scary but not enough to get Clay to move back.

Instead, he latched onto the wound. Blood hit his tongue, making him shudder. He wrapped his legs around Rowan and used the hold to pull him closer. Something happened, and Clay could feel their bond for the first time.

He was human, so until now, he'd only felt drawn to Rowan, but he hadn't been able to feel the bond. Now that he could, it amazed him. The bond was full of pleasure and need, all of it running in a loop between them that grew stronger as the seconds ticked by.

And then, it was complete. It almost felt like it snapped into place, even though it had always been there. Whatever the case, the bond had connected, and pleasure coursed through it. Clay had never come without touching his cock, but between the bond and the friction of his and Rowan's stomachs rubbing together and trapping it, he didn't have to. His body tightened, and he pushed his head back as he screwed his eyes shut.

Clay hoped there was no one in the rooms around the one he and Rowan shared, because if there was, they'd know what had just happened. He couldn't find it in himself to care, though. He held Rowan as he shuddered, and without asking, he knew Rowan had come, too. For a moment, neither of them moved. They breathed against each other's mouths, and Clay felt something settle deep inside of him, almost as if the bond was settling in and making space for itself.

When Clay opened his eyes, it was to see Rowan peering down at him. His mate looked younger and softer. If this was the only thing Clay could ever give Rowan, he'd be fine with it. He wanted to be the one person Rowan felt comfortable with, the one place where he could be himself. He wanted to take away the pain Rowan had endured all these years.

And maybe Rowan could do the same for him.

CHAPTER FIVE

Rowan was living the life he'd always wanted but had never thought he'd have. He had a mate, and they were bonded. He had a family again, and while he'd always miss his parents and his siblings, spending time with Emery and his family soothed the pain their loss had left behind. Not everything was perfect in Rowan's world, but it was damn near close, and he'd do anything he could to protect the people he loved.

That included hunting.

He'd kept himself away from the Krsnik community for the past twenty years. He had no idea how many Kudlaks were around, but he knew how dangerous they were. Many Krsniks had died over the decades, and Rowan was worried that it seemed humans were the only ones left fighting the Kudlaks. It wasn't their job or their destiny. They shouldn't be dying to do something Rowan was born to do.

He looked at Hazel and Matthew, who were playing on the floor. Right now, they were safe in Whitedell, but eventually, they'd grow up. They'd become adults, and they'd want to explore the world. What if a Kudlak found them? Hazel was a full harpy, but Matthew was half Krsnik. If a Kudlak found him, they wouldn't hesitate to hurt him, or worse, and Rowan wouldn't be able to live with himself if something happened to him. There was also Aaron, Emery's oldest son. Rowan hadn't met him yet, but he was an adult and was raising his mate's siblings along with him. He needed to be kept safe, too.

"Those are heavy thoughts," Emery said from beside

Rowan. "And for some reason, I don't think they're good thoughts."

Rowan grimaced. "Not at all, unfortunately. I was thinking that I've kept myself away from the Krsnik community and that it probably wasn't the best idea."

Emery nodded and looked at his children. "I did the same in the beginning. I'm still not very involved because I don't want to go back to that life, but I know enough."

"How much of a danger are the Kudlaks?"

"From what I last heard, they're growing in number, and even more worrying, they've started to organize."

Rowan leaned back. "Organize?" Kudlaks always hunted alone. Sometimes, there were two of them, usually mates. Even so, they often managed to hurt or kill the Krsniks attacking them, so Rowan could only imagine how much worse it would be if they moved in groups.

"I haven't seen it myself, but yes. I heard of a group of them, probably around ten, living a few towns over. I've been keeping an eye on them, and I'm pretty sure there are at least a few human hunters keeping them in check, but yes. It's a worry. I'm lucky that the mansion is big and that the pride has a massive territory, because it means my children are free to roam while being safe, but I'm scared. If those Kudlaks find out about me and that I'm here, they might attack."

Rowan tightened his hands into fists, digging his nails into his palms. "I won't let them hurt you."

"I can still protect my family, even though I haven't hunted in a long time."

"I don't doubt that, but you shouldn't have to go out there and hunt. You need to stay here with your family and protect them from the inside."

Emery looked at Rowan. "While you go out there?"

Rowan swallowed. "I don't want to hunt, but it's a necessity, and I won't let anything stop me. I stayed away from hunting for a long time because I'd had enough of the violence. I didn't have a reason to continue going after Kudlaks because they'd taken everything from me. Now, I have you and your family and Clay."

"And he's not going to stay back and stop hunting."

"I always knew that. I knew it when I agreed to give him a chance and when I decided I wanted to bond with him. I'll be fine."

"I know you will. You were always a great hunter."

"So were you, but you have better things to focus on now. I'll keep our family safe. I just need you to be here to welcome me back once I'm done."

Emery grabbed Rowan's hand and squeezed. "Always."

And that was all Rowan needed. He didn't enjoy the violence and wasn't looking forward to going back out there to hunt, but he'd do what was necessary. If a Kudlak was dangerous, Rowan would ensure they couldn't attack or hurt anyone again. He wouldn't kill indiscriminately the way some human hunters did, but he'd do his part.

"Just promise you'll call me every morning after you're done hunting," Emery said. "If you don't, I'll come to find you myself. I can't lose you after just getting you back."

"I'll call you as often as you need me to. Besides, you just said there was a group of Kudlaks a few towns over. That's not too far."

"And you could stay here with the pride when you're not hunting."

"I don't think Clay and I will want to move in, but we could find a place in Whitedell."

"If that's what you want, I'll help. You don't have to decide everything today or even tomorrow. As long as you know that you have me and my family, go out there and live your life."

Rowan had an incentive to come back from the hunt now.

He wouldn't abandon his niece and nephews.

Or Emery.

"And I think you should contact the council," Emery continued. "They already have enough work without having to focus on the Kudlaks, and besides, that's kind of our job. I'm pretty sure they'll be willing to pay you handsomely for hunting Kudlaks, and it might even help you start a new clan."

Rowan's stomach churned. "I can't be the head of a clan."

"I don't know who better than you, but if you don't want to, that's fine."

Krsniks lived in villages and called themselves clans. Usually, it was formed by a handful of Krsnik families and other supernatural creatures, including Vile, the fairies who taught Krsniks magic. Emery and Rowan's clan had vanished long ago, and Rowan didn't know if he could revive it. He wasn't sure he had it in him to guide people that way, but it was certainly something to consider.

"I'll contact the council," he agreed. "If you or your alpha could point me the right way, I'd be grateful."

"You should talk to Dom. He's a council member, so he can help. Considering everything I told him, he'll be the first on board with this idea of funding you and Clay to hunt. He's been worried about the Kudlaks being so close to the mansion, and we've already talked about it a few times. He'll be happy to know someone's doing something about it." Emery hesitated. "I'm worried. I don't want to lose you again."

Rowan couldn't make promises. "I'll do my best. Besides, I'm not hunting alone. Clay will be with me."

"I know. It's still scary."

It was. Rowan had every intention of making it out alive and, eventually, retiring. He wouldn't be able to get Clay away from the hunt until Clay found the Kudlaks who'd killed his family, and thinking they never might scared Rowan, but if it came to it, he'd force Clay to retire. He wasn't fooled by his mate. He knew that Clay's knee hurt in the morning where he'd been wounded during a fight. He could see that sometimes Clay was in pain because of old scars. Clay was only twenty-five, and now that they were bonded, he'd live at least another hundred years.

That was, if he didn't go down in a hunt, but Rowan wouldn't allow that to happen.

"We'll do this together, even though I won't be in the field," Emery declared. "I can do some work from here. I can be your liaison with the council and poke around to find information about where the Kudlaks might be. I can be there for you if you need help. Hell, the entire pride will be there for you if you need anything."

While Rowan and Clay weren't pride members, the pride considered them family because of Emery. It was a lot of people, which also meant it was a lot of help if they ever needed anything.

And they would. Rowan knew all too well how hunting Kudlaks was. Eventually, they'd need support, and they'd get it this time.

"It would be nice for Emery to have Rowan closer," Troy said, not looking at Clay but rather outside the kitchen window.

Clay had no doubt he was poking around to find out whether he and Rowan were willing to move to Whitedell. Clay didn't have a problem with that. As long as he had Rowan, he'd be fine.

He suspected Rowan needed this. Rowan had believed his entire family was dead for a long time. Even with Clay now in his life, he needed to be close to Emery. He needed to be reminded that he wasn't alone and that like Clay, Emery wasn't going anywhere. Being closer to Emery and his children would make things easier on Rowan, which was what

Clay wanted.

After Rowan had wanted them to bond, Clay had known they'd hunt together. There was no way out of it for either of them, and not just because Clay wanted revenge. He was planning to kill the Kudlaks who'd killed his family, but beyond that, he wanted to keep the few people he cared about safe. That included the pride, and since Emery had mentioned there was a group of Kudlaks not far from here, Clay had been itching to take them on. He was eager to hunt with Rowan and see him in action again, but he'd known it would be better to give Rowan some time and space. He'd just gotten Emery back, and the two of them deserved to have some time together.

"I don't think we can move in with the pride," Clay told Troy.

"I didn't want to move in with the pride initially, either. It was weird. This many people living under the same roof? I thought there was no way it could work."

"Yet it seems to have for you."

Troy smiled and put his cup of coffee on the counter next to a lopsided and very pink cake. "It wasn't easy, but it does work now. Emery and I have been through a lot. He always believed he didn't have anyone left, and sometimes, I didn't feel up to being the center of his universe. It felt like a daunting task, and I didn't know if I would be enough."

Clay leaned back in his chair, his own cup of coffee in his hand. He'd refused a slice of cake even though Troy had assured him that Nysys had become quite good at baking. He didn't trust the pinkness of the thing. "Because you're human?"

Troy cocked his head. "What makes you think I am?"

Clay blinked. "You know, I'm not sure. I guess I assumed, but I shouldn't have, especially since I saw your daughter sprout wings. As far as I know, Krsniks don't have wings, although I could be wrong." Clay had only ever seen Rowan in his human form, so anything was possible.

"You're not. Krsniks don't have wings in any of the forms they shift into. Hazel isn't our biological daughter, so she didn't get her wings from either of us. Aaron and Matthew do, though. I'm part harpy."

Clay didn't know much about the supernatural world beyond what he needed to know about Kudlaks. He had the basics down like everyone, but that was about it. "Aren't harpies usually female?" That was pretty much all he remembered.

"They always are. I wasn't born a harpy. I was born human."

Clay's mind spun. "You were turned into a harpy?"

"In one of the labs," Troy said with a nod.

He took another sip of coffee as if he was trying to distract himself from the memories. If what he was saying was true, Clay could understand why. He knew about the labs — everyone did — and he could only imagine what Troy had gone through.

"I was lucky I had Emery, but it wasn't easy when I first got here. I'd just found out I wasn't human anymore, and when I got pregnant with Aaron, things got dicey for a while. I wouldn't be here now if I hadn't had Emery and the pride."

Clay had so many questions, but it would be rude to ask them. He was fine with keeping them to himself. He and Troy were family through Rowan and Emery, and eventually, Clay would find out everything about Troy being pregnant.

"I guess that what I'm trying to say is that even when you think it would be best if you were alone, that usually isn't true," Troy explained. "Everyone needs a family, be it the one you were born into or a family you found along the way. We need people who support us, who are there for us when we need help. Emery wants to be that for you and Rowan. We both know you'll be out there hunting soon, and it scares him, but he realizes he can't do anything to stop you. He just wants to be reassured that you'll come home to him and the rest of the family once you're done."

"Well, I can't make promises, but I don't see why we shouldn't come back. I don't have anyone left. My family was killed, which is the main reason I became a hunter. I'd never take the only family Rowan has away from him, so I guess you can expect to see us often."

"That's all we want," Troy said, a smile reappearing on his face.

Clay was starting to realize that all he wanted was to make Rowan happy. For the first time since his family had died, something was more important than finding the Kudlaks who'd killed them. Clay wasn't quite sure what to make of that, but he'd decided to give himself time.

He wasn't opposed to moving to Whitedell and building a life here with Rowan. He wasn't yet ready to stop hunting, but for the first time, he could see himself having a life when he did. Before, he'd thought he'd die a hunter. Now, he knew he'd do everything he could so that didn't happen. He wanted to die as Rowan's mate when they were old and frail.

The conversation with Troy had been a lot to take in, but it had also been good. Clay hadn't entirely realized how lonely he was, even when he was with people. Usually, they were hunters or people that Clay had no intention of having as a family ever again, so he never allowed himself to get close to anyone. Troy was different, as was Emery. They'd be part of Clay's future, and it thrilled him to have someone to come back to once he was done fighting.

He and Rowan met in the room they'd been staying in. Clay suspected Rowan had had a conversation with Emery like he had with Troy. Rowan looked much more relaxed but also determined, and Clay couldn't help but grin.

"What's next?" he asked.

"Emery mentioned that group of Kudlaks a few towns over," Rowan said. "I think we should check them out, just to make sure they won't hurt the pride."

Clay had to resist the urge to kiss Rowan, but then he realized he didn't have to. Rowan was his mate, and they were bonded. So he hooked an arm around Rowan's waist and pulled him close, his smile widening at the squeak that came from his mate. Clay smothered the sound with his lips, and Rowan groaned and leaned against him.

As much as Clay wanted to do more than kiss, they had things to do, so eventually, he took a step back. "You want to hunt," he said.

"It's not that I *want* to."

"But you want to keep your family safe, and you're going to do that through hunting. I understand." And Clay really did. These people might not be his family, at least not by blood, but they mattered to his mate, and his mate mattered to him. That was all he needed to go out there and hunt.

"I'm just worried because we don't know much about them," Rowan said as he started packing. "Like how many Kudlaks live together? They don't usually do that, so I wouldn't know where to start with that bit of information."

"I have an idea, actually," Clay said. He'd already packed this morning, so he didn't have much to do.

Rowan stopped to look at him. "Of course you do. Come on, tell me while I finish here."

Clay was happy to do so. "I usually hunt alone, but not just. Especially in the past few years, it's become more common to find groups of Kudlaks living together and even worse, hunting together. So when I need to, I partner with other hunters. Some of them live nearby, and I thought we could contact them and see if they have any information about these Kudlaks or any Kudlak in the area."

"These hunters are all human?" Rowan asked.

"Yeah. And I don't think any of them has ever met a Krsnik. They know about you guys, but we all thought you were pretty much extinct."

"In the area, I think that was the case. I know of some clans around in the country, but our numbers have been dwindling for decades. It's a hard life, and we usually die young."

"Which is why us humans stepped in. Come on, let's go. I want you to meet these people, and I want to hunt with you." And once they were done, they could find a place to call home and settle down.

For the first time, Clay wasn't terrified of what the future would bring because it would have Rowan in it.

Saying goodbye wasn't easy, but Rowan knew he was doing the right thing, at least when it came to leaving Emery behind. Emery had a family here, and Rowan would never demand he go with him on a hunt, even though it would be safer. No, he'd be the one to protect Emery and his family, and that was perfectly fine with him. Besides, he'd be back in Whitedell soon.

He'd talked to Dominic, who'd seemed eager to welcome him and Clay and even more to give them space to build a new clan. Rowan wasn't sure he could, and he didn't want to because it was too many responsibilities, but he'd promised to keep it in mind. Beyond that, Dominic had confirmed that even if Rowan never wanted a clan, he and Clay would always be welcome with the pride. Something told Rowan that, eventually, he wouldn't be able to continue saying no to building a new clan, but for now, he was fine alone with Clay.

Even though they wouldn't be alone for long.

Rowan was worried about these humans. He had nothing against humans in general, and some, like Clay, were good hunters. The problem was that more often than not, they hunted Kudlaks for revenge. Kudlaks were cruel and didn't hesitate to kill entire families, like they had with Clay and Rowan. Something like that happening to a human was enough to push them into wanting revenge, but what they did with those feelings was the most important thing. Some of them turned that need into something productive, but others couldn't see beyond the need for blood. Rowan had seen human hunters kill shifters who didn't have anything to do with Kudlaks. Hell, he'd even seen hunters kill other humans. He didn't trust the people he and Clay were going to meet, but he might not have a choice when it came to working with them.

He supposed he was about to find out.

"You'll like them," Clay said as he drove.

Since he knew where they were going, that was what made the most sense. Rowan didn't particularly enjoy allowing someone else to be in control, but this wasn't just someone else. It was Clay.

"I mean, you'll like some of them," Clay continued, his focus firmly on the road. "Some can be dickheads, but I'll tell you who so you can stay away from them. Cornelius is the leader and can be a bit of an asshole, but he's a good hunter. I'm not saying you'll like him, but I'm sure he'll be happy to meet you. He knows about Krsniks, so he'll know what you can do and how much you can help."

"As long as he doesn't try to kill me."

"Why would he try to kill you? You're a Krsnik. You were literally born to kill Kudlaks."

"Some people don't see a difference between Krsniks and Kudlaks. Think about it. We're similar, down to the fact that we can turn into various animals and drink blood. The main difference between us is that I turn into a white animal when I shift, while Kudlaks turn into a black one."

"And there's the fact that you're not going around killing

people," Clay added dryly.

"There is that, but some people don't care."

"Well, these hunters do. They'll want you on our side, so they won't do anything to hurt you."

Rowan wasn't too worried about that, although he could be badly hurt if an entire group of hunters came after him. He worried about how many victims these hunters had left in their wake. Were all of them Kudlaks? More importantly, had all of them been cruel killers?

Rowan had lived too long not to know that some Kudlaks weren't like the others. It would have been easier for him to ignore that and kill any Kudlak he encountered, but he'd seen his fair share of cruel hunters, and not just humans. Krsniks could be cruel, too, even though he didn't like to admit it. Some of them killed indiscriminately, but that had never been the kind of hunters Rowan and his family were.

The problem was that Rowan wasn't sure he could get the humans to see reason. Hopefully, he wouldn't have to. He didn't want Clay to be disappointed, and even more importantly, he didn't want anything to happen to either of them. They were going to have to trust these hunters, but Rowan wasn't sure he could, which could become a problem.

The drive wasn't long. Rowan was curious about the area, so he spent most of the time in the car staring out the window. If he and Clay were going to move here, he wanted to be familiar with what was around him. Everything looked nice, but just like in every other place, some areas of the small towns they drove through had seen better days. This was where the Kudlaks liked to hide during the day and when they needed a place to heal, and Rowan started to get anxious. Things didn't get better when Clay parked in front of what looked like an abandoned warehouse.

Rowan turned to him. "What is this place?"

"The hunters live here. Yeah, I know, it's not great, but

there are too many of them to be able to live in an apartment or something like that. I guess they thought this would be the easiest way for all of them to be together. Besides, they don't have a lot of money. They do odd jobs here and there, but their main focus is hunting."

Rowan understood the hunters wanting to stick together. Krsniks lived in clans, and it was all he'd ever known until his family had been killed. The problem with the way these hunters lived was that from what Rowan could tell, every single person here was a hunter. That wasn't the case for clans, which was what made them sustainable. Some clan members were hunters and went out to kill Kudlaks, while others stayed back and took care of the clan. They earned money, kept everyone safe, and gave the hunters a safe place to call home and to come back to. Having only hunters wouldn't have worked, and the imbalance of these human hunters worried Rowan.

But many things worried him at the moment, and there was nothing he could do about any of them, so he pushed those thoughts back and followed Clay out of the car.

Clay didn't hesitate. He strode toward one of the doors, quickly knocking. There was a rhythm to the knock, probably a code to tell whoever was inside that he was a friend.

Eventually, Rowan heard footsteps. He tensed, not knowing what to expect, and got ready to defend Clay if he needed to. The door swung open, and a woman peered out. Her eyes widened, and she pushed the door completely open. "It's been a while," she said, quickly hugging Clay. "I'll be honest, I thought you might be dead. You shouldn't wait so long before contacting us."

"I didn't mean to, but I was busy." Clay looked back at Rowan. "Rachel, this is my mate, Rowan."

She grinned, seemingly happy for Clay, and Rowan relaxed. He didn't think she was one of the bad hunters, and he hoped he wouldn't be wrong.

"Really?" she asked, looking from Clay to Rowan. "That's great. It also explains why you disappeared for so long. Come on in. Cornelius will be happy to see you."

They followed Rachel into the warehouse. She closed and locked the door behind them, and Rowan did his best to ignore the feeling of being locked in. If things got bad, he could fight his way out, or even shift.

The inside of the warehouse wasn't any better than the outside. It was somewhat clean, but it was clear these hunters didn't have a lot of money. Rowan could hear the sound of people fighting, so he wasn't surprised when Rachel led them into a wide, open space in the middle of which two men were fighting. Others were gathered around them, watching them and yelling, trying to push the fighters into hitting harder. They were already going at it hard enough, and blood dotted the ground under their feet and dripped down their faces.

Rowan swallowed. He'd been wary before, and now, he knew he'd been right to feel that way.

Clay had expected Cornelius to be right in the middle of it, and he wasn't wrong. The leader was slightly to the side, watching the fight, his focus moving from one fighter to the other. He didn't yell tips or try to help, but Clay had no doubt he was judging both the fighters.

"Cornelius!" Rachel called out.

Cornelius turned, and his eyes widened when he saw Clay. A smile started forming on his lips until he noticed Rowan. Then the smile was gone, a hard expression taking its place. It was a bit puzzling, but it was probably because Rowan was a stranger and Cornelius didn't know him.

"It's been a while," Clay said when he reached Cornelius.

He grabbed Cornelius's forearm and squeezed, and

Cornelius squeezed back, but he was still staring at Rowan. It was almost as if he couldn't look away, and it made Clay slightly uneasy.

"Rowan, this is Cornelius, the leader of this bunch of hunters. Cornelius, this is Rowan, my mate and a Krsnik."

Rachel sucked in a breath, but Cornelius didn't react. He continued staring at Rowan, and Rowan stared at him. It was almost like a standoff, and Clay wanted to break it.

"Krsniks are extinct," Cornelius said.

"Since I'm standing in front of you, it's obvious they're not," Rowan answered.

"It would have been easy for you to tell Clay you're a Krsnik. Where's the proof that you are?"

Rowan grinned, exposing his fangs. "Why would you need proof? You have Clay's word. Don't you trust him?"

Clay cleared his throat. "Of course he does. Cornelius, Rowan has agreed to help us. He wants to get back into hunting, which is why we're here. We heard about a group of Kudlaks hiding in the area."

Cornelius shook his head. "We don't need his help. We've been fine doing all of this on our own, and we'll continue doing so. We don't need Krsniks to hold our hands."

Clay was confused but also pissed. "Don't you see? He was born to do this. We've been doing a good job, but we're only human. He's faster, and stronger, and he's been fighting Kudlaks for decades. He could be the difference between us losing and winning." Clay had thought Cornelius would jump on that opportunity, and he didn't understand why that wasn't the case.

"Having fangs doesn't mean he's a Krsnik or that he's good at fighting. I can't believe you let him fool you, Clay." Cornelius sounded dismissive, and Clay had enough.

"He didn't fool me. I saw him fight. I saw him kill a Kudlak. Besides, he's my mate, and we're bonded. I know what

I'm talking about when it comes to him."

Cornelius didn't look happy, and while he never did, Clay could tell there was something more to it. What the fuck was wrong with him? He should be jumping at this opportunity, but instead, he was bitching about Clay being fooled.

"It's okay," Rowan said.

But it wasn't. Clay was grateful that, at that moment, the fight ended. One of the hunters had the other on his stomach on the ground, and Cornelius turned to them. He left Clay and Rowan behind, and Rachel followed him, looking hesitant and apologetic.

Clay was glad to have a moment alone with Rowan, and he quickly apologized. "I'm sorry. I don't know what's gotten into him. I thought he'd be happy to have you here."

Rowan shrugged. Thankfully, he didn't look bothered. "I understand why he isn't."

"Do you? Can you tell me? Because I have no clue what's happening."

"He's the leader, right?"

"Yeah."

"And everyone here is human?"

"Unless they picked up someone else while I was gone, yeah."

"Then look at things from his point of view. He's human, and he's been guiding these hunters for a while. Now here comes a Krsnik, who, like you said, was born to hunt Kudlaks. It would make sense for Cornelius to be afraid that I might try to take his place as the leader. I'm uniquely qualified to do so, and he feels threatened."

Clay hadn't thought about that, but he supposed it did make sense.

"There's also the fact that he's in love with you," Rowan added.

Clay spluttered. "What are you talking about?"

"I'm not surprised you didn't notice, because you're so focused on hunting and ignore everything else, but yes. It's pretty obvious that he's in love with you."

"Cornelius isn't in love with anyone. He lives to hunt."

"Well, I beg to differ. He's definitely in love with you, but I'm not surprised he never admitted it. He probably thought he had time, and now that I'm in the picture, he knows he lost you."

Rowan was the person Clay trusted the most in the entire world, so instead of dismissing his words, he took some time to think about them. Could Cornelius actually be in love with him? It felt absurd, but Rowan wasn't wrong when he'd said that Clay was focused on the hunt. He didn't have relationships. Hell, he barely even had sex, and he didn't miss it that much, or at least, he hadn't missed it until meeting Rowan.

But Clay had never wanted anything with Cornelius. He liked the man well enough, but not that way. He couldn't even think about having sex with the guy.

He groaned and rubbed his face. "Did I just ruin all of this?"

Rowan reached out and squeezed Clay's hand. "You didn't ruin anything. Whether or not Cornelius agrees to help us, we'll find these Kudlaks and ensure they never hurt anyone. We don't need these people."

They might not *need* the hunters, but it would be better if they had their help or at least their cooperation. Things could go very wrong if the nest they wanted to investigate had more than a few Kudlaks, and Clay wasn't willing to put Rowan in danger. He'd told Emery and Troy that they would both come back, and he intended to keep that promise.

Clay looked around. Cornelius was making a point of not looking at them, but they'd gotten the attention of more than a few hunters. Clay could count at least a dozen who kept peeking at them, and it gave him hope. Most were probably curious and wouldn't want to go against Cornelius, but Clay had spent time with these people. He wasn't sure he'd call any of them friends, but they'd trusted him with their lives before, so maybe, they'd at least listen to him.

He cleared his throat. "Everyone, this is Rowan, my mate. He's a Krsnik."

Now even the people who hadn't been interested in Clay and Rowan were staring. Clay grinned and ignored Cornelius, who was glaring.

"Yes, I know. We believed they were extinct, but they're not. Rowan lost his entire family to the Kudlaks, and he's ready to help us keep this area safe."

"We don't need his help," Cornelius snapped. "If his entire family is dead, they must not have been good hunters."

Rowan's back went rigid. Clay wondered if he was about to attack. He wouldn't have been surprised after what Cornelius had just said, and to be honest, he might have gotten in a punch or two himself.

"How many people did you lose?" Rowan asked, his voice deceptively soft. "How long have you been hunting? Five years? Ten? And over that time, how many hunters have you watched die? Because I've been fighting Kudlaks for over forty years, and anyone who dies by their hands is a hero. Or do you think your human hunters who died weren't good hunters?"

Cornelius's cheeks flushed. "They were humans. You're supposed to have been born to do this."

"And I have, which is why I've been fighting Kudlaks for forty years next to your five. As far as experience and expertise, I think it's clear who has more of it."

Clay was impressed and had to resist the urge to kiss Rowan. Not only had Rowan put Cornelius in his place, but he'd also explained why every hunter in the building should trust him when it came to Kudlaks.

Chapter Six

Rowan had had his reasons to stop being a hunter. They were good reasons, and he was glad he hadn't forced himself to get revenge and continue hunting when he wanted nothing more than to die with his family. It would have been a disaster because he was pretty sure that if he'd done this twenty years ago, he would have allowed a Kudlak to kill him eventually. He'd been desperate and alone and hadn't had anything to live for.

But things were different now. He wasn't alone anymore. He had a reason to be careful when he hunted and to go home once the hunt was over. Clay had given him a reason to live, and Emery had confirmed that Rowan wasn't alone. It was all Rowan had wanted, and now that he had it, he needed to keep all of it safe.

He hadn't thought Cornelius would agree to have him and Clay hanging around. He'd expected to be kicked out, especially after he'd told Cornelius he was nothing more than a child playing hunter. Those hadn't been Rowan's words, but it was what he'd implied, and he believed it. Cornelius might be the leader of the group of hunters, but he had no idea what he was doing, even though Rowan had no doubt he'd killed his fair share of Kudlaks. Everyone was lucky for a time, but Rowan wouldn't be surprised when Cornelius's luck ran out.

Probably not anytime soon, since Rowan had noticed that Cornelius didn't go out on hunts often. He preferred to send others, which again wasn't a surprise. He used his role as a leader to keep everyone under control and act as if he was better, but like everyone here, he was scared.

There was no shame in being scared. Every time Rowan went out, he was afraid. He'd shared that with the hunters he and Clay had been working with, and they'd all been surprised, but Rowan thought it was a good thing. Fear was normal, and acting as if one wasn't afraid could only lead to trouble.

"What do you think?" Clay asked, knocking his shoulder against Rowan's.

Rowan looked at the hunters fighting in the middle of the warehouse. This was a regular occurrence, which he didn't fully understand. He understood needing to train and agreed with it, but why make a spectacle out of it? To his eyes, it only served to set hunter against hunter, which wasn't what they needed.

But it was none of his business. He wasn't the leader, and he had no intention of taking that away from Cornelius. If these people wanted to follow that man's orders, they were welcome to do just that.

But watching Cornelius and his hunters had made Rowan think about creating a new clan. Not all the hunters were happy with how Cornelius did things, and they'd started to gravitate toward Rowan and Clay. Rowan wouldn't be surprised if those hunters decided to leave with them eventually, which meant he'd have to be careful when it came to Cornelius, who wouldn't take it well. It also meant he might have to talk to Dominic again about the pride giving a part of its territory to welcome the clan.

This mess made Rowan's head hurt.

He turned his attention to Clay, who, like him, was watching the fight. "She's better," he said.

Clay grinned. "She always was. I swear some of these guys think that just because Rachel is a woman, she can't kick their ass. They never learn."

"You've known her a while."

"There's no need to be jealous. There was never anything between us because I'm very much gay."

Rowan grinned. "I'm not jealous. I'm your mate."

"Which makes you the most important person in my life." Clay glanced at the fight again.

Rachel clearly had the upper hand, and it was honestly becoming kind of boring. Cornelius was yelling at the man Rachel was fighting, trying to give him pointers, but it was useless. If that guy was like this in a fight with another human, Rowan couldn't imagine what he was like facing a Kudlak. It could get better if the guy trained the right way, but Rowan doubted that would ever happen with Cornelius in charge.

He sighed. "These people need help," he murmured.

"I never realized it until you showed me, but you're right. Cornelius has been in charge for long enough that no one wants to rock the boat, but he's not good for them. He's going to get someone killed." Clay grimaced. "I'm pretty sure he's already gotten someone killed. I know these aren't your people, but we can't leave them here."

"I doubt Cornelius is forcing them to stick around."

"He's not, but most of these people have nowhere else to go. They all lost family or someone they cared about, and they didn't know what to do. Cornelius is taking advantage of that. He's made them think there isn't another place for them in the world, and I don't like that. I should have seen it sooner."

Rowan quickly squeezed Clay's hand. "It wasn't your fault. You were focused on your mission and thought they were in good hands. You've never spent long periods of time with them, have you?"

"No. I'm usually in and out as soon as the hunt is over."

"Then you couldn't know."

"But now, I do. I don't know if I can leave them behind."

Rowan turned toward the fight, not at all surprised to see

Cornelius glaring at him. He'd been doing it since the moment Rowan had arrived, and it got worse every time Rowan touched Clay. Clay hadn't believed Cornelius was in love with him before, but he hadn't been able to deny it after seeing how Cornelius behaved. It was making things awkward, but they had more important things to focus on than Cornelius's hopeless crush on Clay.

Cornelius turned his attention back to the fight. "Come on," he yelled. "What are you, a sissy? Kick her ass."

Rowan tensed. He understood why Cornelius wanted to push his hunters, but that wasn't the right way to do so.

"I think we should stop," Rachel said.

"We're not stopping until he finally man's up," Cornelius snapped at her. "Beat her ass," he ordered the man.

Rowan had had enough. He was pretty sure Rachel could beat the guy she was fighting unconscious, but that wasn't what anyone here should want. When he glanced around the room, he could see that most of the hunters were uncomfortable with what was happening. None of them would stand up to Cornelius, but he didn't care about Cornelius's feelings or what he thought of him. He didn't care if Cornelius kicked him out. This wasn't his home, and these weren't his people.

"That's enough," he said. He didn't yell, but he still got everyone's attention.

Rachel looked relieved and took a step back. The man she was fighting slumped on the ground, the fight clearly over for him. Another man rushed to his side, crouching next to him and putting a hand on his shoulder.

"What the fuck did you say?" Cornelius said, storming toward Rowan.

Rowan didn't back down. "You heard me. The fight's over."

"You can't give my people orders."

"I'm not giving anyone orders. It's clear that this guy won't beat Rachel. Why are you doing this? This isn't the right way to train them."

"What would you know about how I should train my hunters? You hunt alone."

"I might now, but I was born into this. I was trained to be a hunter since I was a child, so like everything else when it comes to hunting, I have more experience than you. This isn't the way to do this."

Cornelius kept some distance between them, probably because he was afraid Rowan would kick his ass. He wasn't cowed, though—not that Rowan had expected him to be.

"You have experience, you say," Cornelius spat out. "Well, let's see it. I found that nest you were asking about. Why don't we all head out so we can see how good of a hunter you are?"

Rowan exchanged a glance with Clay, who'd been standing by his side the entire time. This might not be the way he wanted to do things, but he'd needed to find the nest, and Cornelius had been keeping the information from him, probably hoping he would eventually leave to find the Kudlaks himself. If he thought he'd intimidate Rowan into saying no to going to the nest, he couldn't have been more wrong.

Rowan grinned at him, making sure to expose his fangs. "Lead the way."

Clay wasn't sure this was the best idea. Cornelius had been pushing Rowan, and while Rowan had ignored him until now, that seemed to be over. Cornelius clearly hadn't expected Rowan to agree to go to that nest, but he had, and they were headed there.

It was what Clay and Rowan had wanted. Clay was relieved they were finally doing this, but he wasn't sure what was about to happen. They didn't have any information on the Kudlaks because Cornelius hadn't told them anything except that he could lead them to the nest. How many Kudlaks would they have to face? Would Rowan be able to fight them? Clay had no doubt his mate would do his best, but he was only one man, even though he'd been born to hunt Kudlaks. Clay didn't like any part of this, and he felt it was partially his fault. He'd been the one to bring Rowan to the hunters and Cornelius. He'd been the one to insist they could help.

And now, they were about to face a nest, and he was terrified for his mate.

He understood better why Rowan had been so opposed to him hunting. Now that they were doing this together, Clay was terrified something would happen to Rowan. He didn't want his mate to be hurt. Rowan knew what he was doing, but knowing that wasn't as helpful as Clay wished it was. There was an inkling of doubt in the back of his mind that told him that something bad might happen to Rowan, and it would be all his fault.

Thankfully, Rowan had declared that he and Clay would take their car. Rowan was driving, following the van in front of them, and while he was focused on the road, it gave them enough privacy in time to talk.

"You're worried," Clay said.

He liked that Rowan didn't hesitate to confirm it. He wasn't hiding his feelings. "I am. Kudlaks don't usually nest."

"I don't know about that. I mean, when I started hunting, I usually found them alone, but over the past few years, I've seen several nests. It makes sense for them, right? The more of them there are, the stronger they are."

"But that's not how it works. Kudlaks hunt alone or with their mate. They don't like sharing their prey, which can often lead to fighting. They're solitary creatures because they kill each other."

"What about families?" Because even though Kudlaks drank blood, they weren't vampires. They were shifters, and as far as Clay knew, they had kids just like Krsniks.

Rowan's jaw tightened. "I've only ever seen young Kud-laks a few times. They're extremely well protected, but even when children are present, it's usually only one of them. That would make three Kudlaks, not an entire nest. They don't have extended families. It's actually a miracle when they have both their parents."

It felt a bit like the same could be said for Krsniks, but Clay didn't say that out loud. Krsniks and Kudlaks were two sides of the same coin—similar, yet at the same time, completely different. Rowan didn't need to be reminded of any of this. He'd grown up in this world and knew better than Clay what he was saying.

"What do you think it means that they've started gathering in nests?" he asked.

Rowan grimaced. "That they're organizing."

"And that's not a good thing." Because they'd been hard enough to fight when they were alone or with their mate. Having to face an entire nest wouldn't be easy, and while Rowan would probably be okay, Clay and the other hunters were human. Hopefully, Cornelius knew what he was doing, but Clay was starting to wonder if that was the case.

They were silent as they continued following the van in front of them. It didn't take long for Cornelius to park, and when he did, Clay looked around.

They weren't that far from the warehouse where the hunters lived. This area was full of what looked like abandoned houses that had seen better days, very much like the warehouse. These were individual houses, but that didn't mean it would be easier for them to defeat the Kudlaks, which worried Clay.

Once, Clay wouldn't have hesitated to rush into this. Now, he couldn't do that. He knew what he and Rowan would face, and he wasn't alone anymore. If he could avoid getting killed, he wanted to do so, and he wanted the same to go for Rowan. He had every intention to retire with Rowan and live the rest of their lives in peace eventually, and that wouldn't happen if one of them got killed.

The hunters started getting out of the van, and Clay and Rowan left the car. Most hunters gave Rowan a wide berth, and Clay had heard what they thought of him. Even though he was a Krsnik and had been born to fight Kudlaks, they didn't like him because he was too similar to Kudlaks. He could shift and drink blood, and to them, that was enough. Clay understood, but he hadn't yet seen Rowan drink blood, and he wondered how much of it he had to drink to survive. What he *had* seen was Rowan eating human food, several times. The hunters had, too, and while Clay hadn't expected them to accept Rowan with open arms, he'd hoped they'd at least realize he was an expert when it came to the hunt. It was one thing not to like him because of what he was. It was another entirely to decide that he didn't know what he was talking about and rush into danger without listening to the expert.

"What do we know?" a woman asked, her attention on Cornelius.

"Three individuals. They'd been staying here a while, and I'm sure they're in there." He looked at Rowan. "So, mister expert? What are we waiting for."

Rowan gave him a wicked grin, then took out two long knives he'd started wearing at his sides. From the way he moved, it was clear he was used to fighting with them. They were an extension of his body, and it was damn impressive.

Also kind of hot.

Cornelius looked like he'd swallowed something sour as he gave orders for the house to be surrounded. He selected a small group of hunters to go into the house itself, and they placed themselves behind Rowan as he reached the front door. Clay wasn't behind him, though. He was right next to him because they were facing this together.

Rowan looked at Clay, who nodded.

"Ready?" Rowan asked.

"Ready," Clay confirmed.

They walked into the house.

Clay's nose instantly started itching because of the dust, but he breathed through his mouth, and the sensation eventually dissipated. He followed Rowan, careful of where he was putting his feet. Rowan gave one look at the stairs then turned away from them. Cornelius snorted somewhere behind Clay, but Clay ignored him. Rowan was right. Unless Kudlaks could fly, there was no way they were up there because the dust on the stairs hadn't been disturbed in a long time. Several of the steps were broken, and it would be dangerous to try to go up there, especially without a good reason to do so.

The house was dark and smelled of mildew. Clay could feel the wind coming in from a broken window, and when he peeked into what had once been the living room, he could see a curtain lazily moving along with it.

Then, his gaze caught something in the corner.

He and Rowan looked at each other. Rowan nodded and stepped into the living room with his knives raised. Someone, probably one of the Kudlaks, had pushed the remaining furniture around to make a nest at the back of the room in the corner. That was all Clay could see. There was a bundle of blankets and a couch placed in front of it. It gave whoever was in the nest some protection from the wind, but it wouldn't be enough to keep Rowan away.

"There they are," Cornelius said behind Clay.

He started to move forward, but Clay thrust a hand out. He glared at Cornelius, who glared right back at him.

"We should set the house on fire," Cornelius said. He

sounded smug, and it gave Clay the chills.

"Please, no," a voice said.

Someone appeared from the nest. Someone else inside the nest tried to stop them, but the person shook their hand off and stepped forward. It looked like a woman from where Clay was, but when the person stopped in front of the window, he realized it was a teenage boy.

Rowan sucked in a breath. "You're human," he said to the boy.

The boy stared at him. "How do you know?"

"I can smell it." Rowan paused. "That means I can also smell the Kudlaks with you in the nest."

The boy opened his arms as if he could shield the Kudlaks. "Don't hurt them, please."

Clay had no idea what to think of this. He'd never heard of Kudlaks living with humans, but that seemed to be what was happening here.

What the fuck?

"Kill the Kudlaks," Cornelius ordered as if Rowan would do anything he said.

Rowan glared at him. "And what about the boy? Do you want me to kill him, too?"

Someone in the nest cried out, and Rowan tensed when they scrambled to get out of the nest. He had to work hard not to show his surprise when a female Kudlak appeared, a child clinging to her chest. She placed herself in front of the human boy, almost as if she was ready to defend him. She probably was, but she wasn't one bit threatening, especially with the child hanging from her neck.

The little girl couldn't be more than three or four, if even that. Rowan could smell that she was a Kudlak, but she wasn't a threat, and from the looks of it, neither was the woman carrying her. Rowan couldn't tell if she was the mother, but if he had to guess, he'd say she was. He wasn't sure what the human boy had to do with this, but he wouldn't do anything rash that could lead to someone getting hurt.

"Please," the woman said.

Her eyes were wide with fear, which Rowan could understand. She wasn't only facing an entire group of human hunters. She was facing a Krsnik, her sworn enemy by birth.

"We'll take the boy," Cornelius said. "He'll make a good hunter. Kill the other two, and we'll set the house on fire so they can never use this place again."

Rowan sucked in a breath and turned to look at Cornelius. His night vision was better than a human's, so he could see some of the hunters looked horrified at his suggestion. He was telling Rowan to kill a mother and her child. The girl was nothing more than a toddler, and while she'd grow up to be an adult Kudlak, this wasn't something Rowan could do. He had enough blood on his hands, and he wasn't planning on adding the blood of a child to it.

He turned toward Cornelius, dismissing the woman and the kids. "You want me to kill a child?"

"She's a Kudlak. I don't care if she's a child or eighty years old. She's dangerous."

"She couldn't hurt a fly right now, and neither could her mother." Rowan could tell she was weak from the way she stood, wavering as if she didn't have enough strength to hold her up.

She'd probably been feeding the children and not eating herself. Rowan was curious about why she had a human boy with her, but now wasn't the moment to ask. Rowan had to deal with Cornelius and possibly with the rest of his people.

"Isn't this what you were born to do?" Cornelius asked, stepping closer and getting right into Rowan's face.

Rowan tightened his hands around his knives to resist the

temptation to stab Cornelius. He didn't have to kill him. He could stab him just a little, and hopefully, it would get Cornelius to shut up.

He wasn't sure he could resist the temptation, so he put away his knives then thought better of it and took one out again, just in case Cornelius continued being an asshole.

"You can't kill a kid," one of the hunters said from behind Cornelius.

Rowan was pretty sure it was Rachel. He was glad she was standing up to Cornelius, but he wasn't sure it would do anyone any good. Cornelius's chest was puffing up, and he was clearly getting ready to yell, which wasn't something Rowan wanted to live through.

"She's not a child!" Cornelius yelled. "She's a monster. If we don't kill her, she'll kill us." He turned back to Rowan. "I knew it. I don't care if you're a Krsnik and were born to do this. You're a Kudlak sympathizer, and we don't tolerate those."

Rowan wasn't afraid. It wouldn't be easy to fight back if all the hunters attacked at once, but he had experience. He could beat their asses, especially with Clay supporting him and kicking ass.

"But clearly, you tolerate having a monster guiding you," he said.

Cornelius didn't like those words. He launched himself at Rowan, clearly not having thought this through. Rowan hadn't planned on fighting with humans tonight, but this was fine.

Maybe he'd get to stab Cornelius after all.

Rowan danced out of the way. He glanced at Clay, who looked worried, but thankfully obeyed when Rowan tilted his chin toward the woman and the kids. Rowan liked that he didn't have to tell Clay what he wanted. Clay moved, placing himself in front of them to protect them. He probably had no idea what was happening, but neither did Rowan. Not knowing what was going on wouldn't be enough for either of them to kill a child.

And clearly, they weren't the only ones. Rachel stepped forward and placed herself next to Clay, standing shoulder-to-shoulder with him. The man she'd beaten during the fight Rowan had interrupted earlier moved to Clay's other side along with his friend. The other hunters looked worried, but Rowan couldn't focus on them.

Cornelius kept coming, and Rowan kept moving out of the way faster than Cornelius could track. Cornelius might be trained, but he'd allowed his emotions to take over, which meant he was easy to fight. He was angry and wanted to pound Rowan's face into the ground. That kind of reaction meant he'd get tired soon and that he'd do something stupid that would allow Rowan to kick his ass.

Rowan couldn't wait.

"Fight me," Cornelius said through gritted teeth.

"Why should I? You're acting like a child having a tantrum."

That made Cornelius angrier. He threw himself at Rowan, and while Rowan got out of the way easily, there was a flicker of pain in his arm. He looked down to see that Cornelius had managed to slash him with his knife. It burned a little, but it was easy to ignore.

But Rowan had enough. Cornelius might be a trained hunter, but he was nothing next to Rowan, especially in this state. Rowan had known that he and Clay staying with the hunters wouldn't be a good idea, and he'd been right. He wasn't sticking around one second longer than it took him to help the Kudlak and the children. Then, he'd be out of there, and he didn't care what happened to Cornelius.

Hopefully, getting his ass kicked would help him realize he needed to reevaluate his life.

The next time Cornelius tried to stab Rowan, Rowan moved forward rather than backward. Cornelius's eyes widened, and when Rowan grabbed his wrist, he cried out. Rowan raised his knee, slamming Cornelius's wrist against it. Cornelius tried to keep the knife, but his fingers spasmed, and he let go. The knife clattered on the floor, and Rowan kicked it aside as he kept his hold on Cornelius's wrist. He moved around the man, twisting his arm until his hand was against his back, with Rowan behind him. From there, he pushed Cornelius forward, slamming him against the wall. A cloud of dust rose around them, and Cornelius tried to fight back, but he was stuck. Rowan leaned heavily against him, pinning him in place.

"Are you done?" he asked.

Cornelius panted. "You said you were on our side, but it was a lie," he spat out.

Rowan pressed him even harder against the wall before letting go. Cornelius twisted and fell back, staring at Rowan. Rowan almost expected him to attack again, but he stayed there, breathing heavily.

Rowan trusted Clay to have his back, so he turned toward the other hunters. "This isn't the way," he said. "I know most of you have lost people to the Kudlaks, and I understand. They killed my family, and if I ever find those who did that, I'll make sure they can never hurt anyone else."

He thrust a finger toward the woman and the kids. "But they had nothing to do with that. That child had nothing to do with it, and while I won't deny that I killed many Kudlaks over the years, I never hurt a child, and I won't start tonight. Wanting revenge and being as bloodthirsty as some of you are will only lead to death and pain. If you kill a child, you'll become monsters like the Kudlaks you're hunting. Is that what you want? Do you want to become like them? Because I don't, and I won't allow Cornelius to push me into anything."

He looked at Clay, who nodded.

"Rowan and I are leaving," Clay said. He moved closer to the woman, and while she still looked terrified, she allowed him to put a hand on her back. "And we're taking these people with us. We won't allow you to hurt them, and if you try, you'll have to contend with Rowan and me."

"And me," Rachel said, her voice strong.

The two guys standing with her nodded, silently telling the other hunters they agreed.

Rowan didn't want to do this, but he also didn't want to leave these people with Cornelius. If they truly wanted to and thought they were doing a good thing, they'd stay, but if they didn't, Rowan would give them an alternative.

"You can stay with Cornelius, or you can come with us," he said, looking at them. "Your choice."

He was done talking, so he turned and headed toward the door.

Clay was really fucking impressed. For all that Rowan had told him that he wanted nothing to do with hunters and didn't want a position of power in their group, he'd taken control of the room in just a few seconds. Clay didn't expect all the hunters to follow him outside, but Rachel did, along with a small group. Clay couldn't focus on them, though.

He gently guided the woman toward the door. Her eyes were wide with fear, but she seemed to be able to tell that following him was the only thing she could do. She walked hesitantly, clutching the child to her chest, the teenage boy standing by her side looking like he was ready to fuck up anyone who tried hurting them.

Clay would be right there with him, helping him do just that.

"I'm Clay," he murmured. "I know you're scared, but we

won't hurt you."

She nodded. "Melissa," she said in a trembling voice. "And these are Devon and Haley."

Clay smiled at the little girl. She was also terrified, which was entirely understandable. "Hi there."

Haley hid her face against Melissa's neck. Clay didn't push, instead turning his attention to Devon. "It looks like you have an interesting story to tell." Why was a human teenager hanging around two Kudlaks? He was protective of them, which probably meant he'd spent a lot of time with them.

Devon glared at Clay, but Clay wasn't offended. He'd have been surprised if Devon had gone along with this with a smile.

"All of you are done with us," Cornelius said from behind Clay. "If you leave, you'll be considered traitors. You'll never have a place with us again."

It wasn't Clay's place to answer, but thankfully, he didn't have to. Rachel did, glaring back at Cornelius. "We don't want a place with you. You were about to kill a kid, and I want nothing to do with that."

"They're Kudlaks," Cornelius insisted.

Clay had had enough. "Stop it," he told Cornelius as he turned around.

"I can't believe you're on his side." Cornelius sounded hurt. "We've been hunting for years. We hunted *together*, yet it's like I never knew you."

"The same goes for me. I understand the need for revenge, and I understand wanting to keep people safe, but this isn't the way. Who will you keep safe by killing a child? And what's next? Once you've killed the child, what will you do?"

"We can't stop hunting."

"We won't." Clay looked around. "I'm not saying Rowan and I are perfect. No one is, and we're not trying to be. But I have experience, and Rowan even more so. We both lost our families to the Kudlaks, so we understand where most of you stand. That doesn't mean we want to become monsters. The little girl has done nothing to hurt any of you. How could you even think about killing a child? Is your need for revenge so important that you're ready to put that kind of mark on your soul?"

"We don't have anywhere else to go," a voice said from the back of the group of hunters who'd stopped behind Cornelius.

Clay gestured at the hunters who'd already placed themselves at his and Rowan's side. "Because they do? Or even me? I'd live on the streets if it meant not having to kill innocent people."

"We're coming with you," Rachel said.

"You can't," Rowan said. He glared at Clay, and Clay knew exactly why.

He'd been resisting the idea of creating a new clan, but Clay had a problem with that. He and Rowan could do good in the world. They could hunt Kudlaks and, at the same time, ensure that those who weren't dangerous weren't hurt. They could train people to do that, watch each other's backs, and make it to retirement. Hunting on their own wasn't going to cut it now that they were together, and Clay had every intention of growing old. They needed more help, and that was what these hunters were offering.

He moved toward Rowan. "They can," he said. "Because if they can't follow you, then who will they follow? You're the best person to lead a new Krsnik clan, and you know it. I understand why you're afraid of the responsibilities and that you could lose these people, too, but it doesn't have to be that way. You're not alone anymore, Rowan. You have me, your cousin, the entire Whitedell pride, and I'm pretty sure you also have Rachel and her friends."

"I'm not a clan leader," Rowan insisted.

"Then I will be," Clay offered. "I mean, I'm used to doing this alone, but I guess I might as well learn to fight with others. You and I make a pretty good team, and I'm sure the same can be said for others."

Rowan scowled. "You're not hunting without me."

"Then do this with me. Be there for these hunters, but also for these Kudlaks. Be there to show people that not all of them are bad and that together, we can try to fix things. It's only our corner of the world, and it's not much, but it'll be everything to someone. Imagine how many families we could stop from being exterminated. We'll never be able to get rid of every evil person in the world, but we can help as many people as possible so they don't have to go through what you and I had to endure. That's what I always wanted, and now that I've met you, I feel closer to that goal than ever. But I can't do it alone, Rowan."

Clay supposed he could have if they hadn't bonded. He could have grabbed his hunters, found a new warehouse to hunker down in, and gone from there. But he and Rowan *had* bonded, and more importantly, Rowan should be the one in charge of this. There was no one better, and Clay wouldn't change his mind about that.

"Where am I supposed to put these people?"

"Call Emery or Dominic. They both told you we could settle down in Whitedell, and they knew it meant creating a clan there. They know we'll need more than just a house, and Dominic mentioned the council paying. You'll have more support than you ever did, even when your family was alive. People need us, Rowan, and I'm not going to turn my back on them. Will you?"

Clay thought he already knew the answer to that question, but he still held his breath. He and Rowan stared at each other, and while Clay was aware he'd probably pushed too hard, he didn't think there was another option to get out of the situation. The hunters were watching them, and he was surprised Cornelius hadn't pitched a fit again, but he seemed to be fascinated by Rowan.

Eventually, Rowan nodded. "Fine. I'll call Dominic and have him contact the council. We'll go from there." He looked at the hunters. "I'm not making any promises. I don't know how to lead a clan, and I'm pretty sure I'll be shit at it, but Clay is right. All of you need a place to call home, and I might have a way to make that happen." He huffed. "So, I guess you should follow Clay and me to Whitedell. If you need anything, you have our numbers. We'll see you there."

Having said that, he climbed into the car. Clay was smiling like an idiot. He'd gotten more than he'd expected, and it was time for them to leave.

But there was still a problem. He looked at the Kudlak and the kids, wondering what they were supposed to do with them. He wasn't about to leave them with Cornelius and his hunters, so he gestured them toward the car. "Come on."

"Where are you taking us?" Devon asked. He looked ready to fuck up Clay if he didn't like his answer.

Clay liked the kid. "Not sure yet. Probably a motel for tonight, and then, we'll go from there."

"You're going to hand us over to the council?"

"That's what you got from all of this? No, we're not handing you over to anyone."

"Will we be part of your clan, then?"

Clay bit his lower lip. "I'm not sure. I don't know much about clans, so I don't know if Kudlaks can be part of them. We'll have to check with Rowan, but in the meantime, we'll keep you safe, whatever happens."

Devon didn't seem convinced, but Melissa nodded and gently pushed him toward the car. Unless he wanted to stay back with Cornelius, Devon had to come along, and Clay was relieved when he did. He was curious about the kid, but he was pretty sure that he wouldn't get a straight answer if he asked. That was fine with him. Devon would tell him what had happened to him and how he'd ended up with two Kudlaks in his own time.

No one tried to stop them from leaving. Cornelius was pissed, but he'd lost too many hunters to do anything about it. Clay wouldn't be surprised if he set the house on fire just because he could, but it was none of his business. Melissa and the kids were out, and that was all that mattered.

"Where do I go?" Rowan asked once Clay was in the car.

"I don't know. Whitedell?"

"All right." Rowan sounded resigned. "But first, we're going back to the warehouse to grab our things."

"You think it's a good idea?"

"If anyone tries to hurt them, they'll have to deal with me."

Rowan sounded fierce, and it made Clay want to drag him to a dark spot to have his way with him. Unfortunately, they were sharing the car with three people who wouldn't want to see that, so he kept his hands to himself. Still, he leaned toward Rowan, needing his mate to know how he felt. "I love you."

Rowan glared. "Shut up and think about the consequences of what you've done."

Clay grinned. He could do that.

He could do anything as long as he was with Rowan.

CHAPTER SEVEN

R owan stared at the scene in front of him. The houses were coming along, and soon, he and Clay would be able to move into theirs. It would be different from the others, which were generic so they could welcome whoever ended up living there. Rowan and Clay had asked for a few specific things before construction began, and Dominic and his people had been more than happy to give it to them.

It was taking some getting used to. After Rowan and Clay had rescued Melissa and the kids, they'd driven straight to the warehouse, then from there, to Whitedell. They'd gotten two rooms in a motel, and Rowan had expected Melissa to be gone the next evening.

She hadn't been. She'd still been in the second room with the two kids, and when Rowan asked where he should take them, she'd shaken her head. He hadn't pushed, but he suspected she didn't have anywhere to go or any other family. It was her, her daughter, and Devon.

Which still puzzled Rowan.

From what he'd learned, Devon had been homeless when he'd stumbled on Melissa and Haley. Melissa had taken pity on him and started taking care of him, and they'd become a family of sorts. He was fiercely protective of them, which was odd because Kudlaks usually killed humans, while humans ran from them.

Melissa wasn't a killer. Rowan hadn't asked for details, but he had no doubt she'd drunk from humans before, at the very least. She'd promised she wasn't out for blood, and Rowan

115

believed her. The kids were her entire life, and she'd done everything she could to ensure they survived. It hadn't always been pretty, but she wouldn't have to worry about that anymore.

Because they were part of Rowan's clan.

Rowan glared at the thought and turned away from the houses. How had he ended up a clan leader? He'd told Clay he couldn't do it, and Clay had been fine with it, but at the same time, he'd pushed Rowan into accepting the role. Dominic had been happy when Rowan called and explained the situation, and he'd put his people to work immediately. He was on the council, and after a few phone calls, he'd confirmed they would be funding Rowan, his hunters, and his clan.

Rowan wasn't sure who would be part of the clan. Usually, it was several families of Krsniks, along with some Vile families, who helped teach magic. That wouldn't be the case for this clan, though. So far, it was Rowan and Clay, Melissa and the kids, and several human hunters who'd trickled in since leaving Cornelius. Rachel had been one of the first, and Rowan had been glad to see her. She was a strong fighter, and she'd come in handy once they started going on hunts again. For now, though, Rowan was focused on Clay and the new clan, and it was more than enough for him.

But Clay missed hunting, which was why Rowan had a surprise for him. He grinned as he headed back toward the mansion. Dominic had been happy to let him and Clay stay there until their place was ready, and Rowan was glad to spend more time with his cousin. It also meant he had to spend more time with the Whitedell pride members, including Nysys, but he was getting used to the guy.

Well, mostly.

He found Clay in the living room with Troy and his son, Matthew. Clay looked up right away as if he felt Rowan coming closer, and maybe he had.

"What did you have planned?" he asked as soon as Rowan came in.

"How do you know I have something planned?"

Clay tapped his chest. "I can feel the anticipation."

It wouldn't be easy to keep secrets from his mate, but Rowan was going to try. "We're going out."

Clay grinned and jumped to his feet. "Great. I'll see you later, Troy."

Troy seemed bemused but nodded, and Clay and Rowan left the room. Clay was almost bouncing on his feet, which made Rowan grin. He'd do pretty much anything to make his mate happy, and apparently, what made Clay the happiest was kicking Kudlak butt.

"Where are we going?" Clay asked.

"I got news from Dominic that a family was attacked last night. Everyone is safe, but they're freaked out because the person who attacked them tried to drink their blood. He wounded a woman, but thankfully, the authorities intervened before he could do anything else."

"It was a Kudlak?"

"They're pretty sure it was. We know the general area, so I thought we could poke around." Rowan didn't know if they'd find the Kudlak still there, but if he hadn't eaten enough yesterday, he'd be prowling for another victim.

And he'd become the victim instead.

Rowan drove since he knew where they were going, and he made sure to park the car far enough away from the house that people wouldn't notice it. He and Clay were silent as they left the car and made their way toward the house. A light had been left on downstairs, but Rowan knew no one was home. He couldn't hear anyone, and Dominic had told him that the family had been moved temporarily.

This part wasn't Rowan's favorite of the hunt, but he and

Clay found a nice spot to sit down while they watched the house. Then they waited.

It was almost one AM when Rowan heard something move in the bushes. He tensed, and Clay did the same next to him. He probably hadn't heard the sound but was reacting to Rowan.

They looked at each other, and Clay nodded. He gestured at Rowan to go to the right while he'd go to the left, but before either of them could move, Rowan's gaze stopped on the Kudlak creeping toward the back door. His world tilted, and he had to reach out to keep himself on his feet. His hand touched a tree, but he could barely feel the bark.

"Rowan?" Clay whispered.

It was enough to get the Kudlak's attention. He turned around, cautious, then grinned when he saw Rowan. Rowan didn't hesitate to push away from the tree and didn't stop when Clay tried to get him to.

He kept his distance from the Kudlak, but he still faced him. He had to because this was the Kudlak who'd killed his family.

"I think I remember you," the Kudlak said.

He was tall and blond, and while Rowan couldn't see his eyes, he knew they were blue. He'd seen his face in drawings and pictures, which was the only reason he knew who this guy was. "You killed my family." All of them except Emery, one by one, as if he were working through a list.

"You're going to have to be more specific than that. I've killed a lot of people."

"The Harper clan," Rowan said, stepping even closer.

For some reason, the Kudlak seemed delighted. "Oh, of course. I'm only missing a few from my family set. Which one are you?" He cocked his head. "You know, it's a pity I haven't eaten because if I had, I'd take you on right here, right now." He clicked his tongue. "But unfortunately, I'm not up for a fight tonight. I'll see you soon, though. Now that I know you're in the area, I want to finish my set."

Rowan threw himself forward, ignoring Clay's yell to stop. The Kudlak was too fast, even though he hadn't eaten today. He shifted into something with wings, and as Rowan watched, he launched himself into the air.

Rowan was ready to shift and go after him, but Clay grabbed his arm. "No," he said.

Rowan tried to pull away. "He killed my family."

"I know, but if you go after him now, you'll lose. You're too angry."

"I might never see him again if I don't follow."

"I'm pretty sure you will. You heard him. Now that he knows you're in the area, he's not going anywhere."

Clay was right. Rowan needed to stop allowing his feelings to do the thinking. He'd heard the Kudlak. The man was staying, and he'd probably come after Rowan. He wanted him dead just because of his family name, but when he tried to kill him, he'd be in for a surprise.

Rowan would be waiting for him.

ABOUT THE AUTHOR

Catherine is the creator of several series, most of them paranormal, including the Whitedell Pride Series and the Gillham Pack Series. While she graduated in translation, she decided to go the writer's way because it was more fun to create her own stories and characters.

She's been living in Italy for more than twenty years, but she's a daughter of the North—Belgium to be precise—and she misses it so much that she's already planning to move back.

She loves pizza—probably too much—her son, her pets, and of course, books. She sneaks some reading time into her schedule every time she has five minutes free from writing, demands from her various pets and son, and lastly, housework.

Connect with her:

lievens.catherine@gmail.com
BookBub: https://www.bookbub.com/authors/catherine-lievens
Website: https://authorcatherinelievens.com/
Facebook: https://www.facebook.com/catherine.lievens.9
Facebook Group: https://www.facebook.com/groups/411788002341528/
Twitter: https://twitter.com/authorCLievens
Newsletter: http://eepurl.com/c-uvKn